BACK TO LIFE

A HARRY MCNEIL NOVEL

JOHN CARSON

FRANK MILLER SERIES

Crash Point
Silent Marker
Rain Town
Watch Me Bleed
Broken Wheels
Sudden Death
Under the Knife
Trial and Error
Warning Sign
Cut Throat
Blood from a Stone
Time of Death

Frank Miller Crime Series box set #1 – Books 1-3

MAX DOYLE SERIES

Final Steps

Code Red

The October Project

SCOTT MARSHALL SERIES

Old Habits

BACK TO LIFE

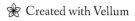 Created with Vellum

For Sylvia Fox Lanspery

ONE

She saw him running down the tight, one-way street and wondered if she should just punch it and run him over. The engine revved harder as she dropped a gear and floored it, the headlights cutting through the cold, dark night, picking him out as he ran down the middle of the road.

The road was slick after the rainfall had thrown leaves onto it, but she didn't care. She didn't take her eyes off him and time was running out.

The road ended down here. They both knew it. That's why he was running harder and she was driving faster.

Then he was on it. The Leamington lift bridge, which did exactly as its name suggested; it lifted the small bridge that spanned the Union Canal so the houseboats could get along to Lochrin Basin.

The man actually stopped in the middle of the bridge for a moment, his breath coming out in plumes like a dragon who couldn't get its fire to work.

There were bollards at either side of the bridge. She didn't know if traffic had crossed here before, or what the deal was, she just knew her car wasn't going across it.

She swung it left and pulled onto the pavement and parked in front of a *Private Parking* sign.

He looked at her and started running again.

She jumped out and looked at him. 'Stop!' she shouted, and slammed the car door when it was obvious he had hearing problems. She took off after him, having the advantage of not being out of breath.

Good shoes, that was the key to running, and actually running on the treadmill and not using it as a clothes horse. She did three miles on it every day before breakfast.

She ran down Gilmore Park to Fountainbridge, gaining on him as she got into her stride. She wished she had thrown her overcoat into the car but it was too late now. She could open it and look like Batman fleeing down the road without a mask on, but she kept it buttoned.

She turned right and saw him. He looked back at her and she was about to cross when a double-decker bus came barrelling along, its tyres hissing on the wet road. The pedestrian crossing light came on and she sprinted over it, her breath coming faster now.

Then she saw him run into the new hotel.

'Gotcha, you bastard,' she said to herself, running along the pavement, almost knocking down somebody who was walking towards her, looking down at his phone.

She ran into the reception but she couldn't see the man anywhere.

'Did you see a man come in here?' she asked the receptionist, her breathing heavy.

'Yes,' the young woman answered.

Sarcastic remarks played through her mind for a moment. 'Where is he?' she asked instead.

'He's a guest.'

She brought out her warrant card and showed it to the woman. 'Where did he go?'

'Room two oh five.'

She walked over to the lift and stood behind an old couple. They all got in and she hit 2 after they'd hit their floor button.

She got off, saw a sign telling her which way the room numbers ran, then walked along to her right. Counted off the door numbers until she got to 205.

She stood, controlling her breathing. She knocked on the door and waited. A few moments later she could sense somebody on the other side.

'Who is it?' a man's voice asked.

'It's me. Open up.'

The door opened and the man she had been chasing stood looking at her before stepping aside. 'Come in,' he said. His own breathing was slowing down.

She stepped into the room and walked towards the bed.

'Can I get you anything?' he asked.

'Water.'

He got two small bottles from the minibar and drank some himself.

'Why did you run?' she asked him after she'd drunk some of the cold liquid herself. Just a sip; she knew the human body could go into shock when overheated then plied with a cold drink.

'I got scared.' His eyes wouldn't settle and he looked around the room.

'Nobody knows about this. You didn't have to run.'

His eyes were wide and his lips trembled for a little bit. He walked slowly towards her. Leant in to whisper something as he pressed the flash drive into her hand.

'Go now. They're waiting.'

'What do you mean?'

'Run!' he shouted, then the bathroom door exploded inwards. The large man in black made to grab her but the man threw himself at the intruder, knocking him aside.

She was opening the door as the two men fell to the floor, then she was in the corridor, the bottle of water dropped. She took the stairs and flew down to the ground floor and out through reception into the cold night air. The lane she'd just run down was across the road.

It was uphill this time and she dug deep, her thighs starting to burn and she knew she shouldn't, but she turned around to look.

Nobody was there.

She got to the top of the road. Her car was just across the way. Across the lift bridge. Safety. Should she just walk and get the car in the morning?

'You look exhausted,' a man said, stepping into view from the canal path. He smiled at her. 'Bit late for jogging, isn't it?'

'Not exactly jogging,' she said, her breath coming in rasps.

'Well, you be careful now. You don't know who's hanging about here at night.'

'I will.'

'People like me,' he said, and she was smacked in the head with a weapon then grabbed from behind, but before she could fight back, she felt the cold, stinging sensation enter her side. She tried to scream, but she couldn't breathe. Her lungs wouldn't work. Then blind panic set in. She thought she was going to be dropped to the ground, but he held her up and was walking her along the canal path like a drunk, still behind her, still with his hand over her mouth. He was bigger and stronger but all the fight had left her.

She walked beside him, her brain screaming for air. Her hand went to her throat but nothing was there. No power, no sensation, no nothing. Just fear.

He still held onto her as he spun her round and then she felt the cold steel enter her front again, over and over and then she could see the stars as she fell backwards.

She didn't feel the cold canal wrap itself around her. She looked up once, but the man wasn't there.

And then there was nothing.

TWO

'Bit nippy for June,' DCI Harry McNeil said, rubbing his hands together.

'You should try flipping your calendar over at the start of each month like me,' DS Alex Maxwell said. 'That way, you'd know it was November the first.'

'Christmas is just around the corner, and I'm in denial.'

They were standing on the edge of the Union Canal along from the end of the ride at Lochrin basin. A grey houseboat was moored along from the Leamington lift bridge; it had been turned into a floating coffee house a while back.

DI Karen Shiels walked up to them. Uniformed officers had secured the footpath, while forensics were scouring the area. A grey mortuary van sat at the end, a harbinger of death.

'Good morning, sir,' Karen said.

'Morning, DI Shiels. What do we have?'

Karen turned to quickly look back at the scene of a fire brigade rescue team standing by a forensics tent that had been hastily erected over the body.

'A female was seen floating in the canal. By the owner of the coffee house there, and he's not best pleased at having his business impacted.'

'I dunno; there's a lot of uniforms here. He might score in the long run.'

'Seems a bit tacky to be selling his stuff to the emergency personnel here, don't you think?' Alex said, shrugging inside her overcoat.

'Well, if he's giving freebies, make mine black with no sugar.' He looked at Karen again.

'The body was between the coffee house and a visiting boat. He called treble nine and a uniform patrol saw her. They thought it might have been a dummy at first, since it was Halloween last night, but on further inspection, they saw it was human.'

'And I'm guessing we're here because it isn't a simple drowning?'

'You guess correctly. The pathologists are over there.'

Harry looked past the fire fighters who were hovering around, and saw one of the mortuary assistants, Angie Patterson, who he had met a few months ago up north. She turned to him and smiled. He smiled back.

'Any ID on her?' Alex asked.

'Yes, her warrant card.'

Harry snapped his attention to Karen. 'She's a police officer? From round here?'

'Yes. Control are getting onto it right now and they'll get back to me.'

'What's her name?'

'Linda Smith.'

'Let me know as soon as you hear something.'

They walked over to where one of the pathologists had just come out of the forensics tent. Dr Kate Murphy, from the city mortuary.

'Good morning, DCI McNeil,' she said with her clipped English accent.

'Morning, doctor. What are we looking at here?'

'Come on, I'll give you the tour.' She walked back into the tent and Harry nodded and smiled at Angie. He had put in a good word with the commander of Edinburgh Division, Jeni Bridge, and she had pulled strings for Marie when she transferred down to Edinburgh, because of her input in solving the case up north.

Jake Dagger, one of the other pathologists, was also in the tent. 'Morning, Harry,' he said.

'Morning, Jake.'

The only other person in the tent was the officer called Linda Smith, lying motionless on a plastic sheet.

'She was found with her overcoat buttoned up, but it has puncture holes in it. They went right through.'

Harry looked down at her. The face looking back at him wasn't familiar. 'Rough idea how long she's been deceased?'

'We're estimating ten to twelve hours,' Dagger said, not using the word *guessing*.

'Between nine and eleven last night,' Harry said out loud, looking at his watch.

'Around that. We'll know a bit better when we get her back to our place and have her dried off properly.'

'Would either of you like to hazard a guess as to what sort of instrument was used to kill her?'

'Something slim,' Kate said. 'Probably a knife, but a long one.'

Harry stepped out into the cold morning air. It had started out with a light frost on the ground. The bowling green opposite his flat had looked like somebody had tried to turn it into a skating rink.

'Uniforms are going door-to-door,' Alex said, coming up to him.

'What about the boats?' he replied, nodding along towards the basin where more houseboats were moored.

'Simon's along there now with the uniforms.' DC

Simon Gregg was another member of his team. Alex turned and looked at the bridge. 'Talk of the devil.'

'You two talking about me?' Gregg said, striding across to them. At six foot six, he towered over them. 'My ears are burning.' He grinned at Alex.

'If your feet move as fast as your mouth, maybe we'll have this solved by lunchtime,' Harry said. 'Tell me what you've got.'

'There's three boats over the other side, all occupied. There's one woman who told me that she's just retired and decided to have a go at living on a boat for a while, but it's getting colder so she's going to leave and go home,' He looked at his notebook. 'Glasgow. And by the look of the boat, she's making the right choice. It looks like a pile of kindling waiting for a box of matches, and it's only a few days 'til Guy Fawkes night.'

'Apart from casting an expert nautical eye over her vessel, anything else stand out? Like, did she hear anything?'

'She did. It was after midnight when she heard a scream. She looked out one of her wee windows, but she thought it was coming from the bar just across the way. She thought nothing of it.'

'That was a bit of a build-up just for nothing,' Harry said, shoving his hands into his pockets.

'Not for nothing, boss. Her little dog, Trixie, goes

for a pee before bed so he doesn't get up in the middle of the night. She was granted shore leave then spent that time sniffing about. She doesn't like the cold, she told me, and was ushering the wee dog along, when a man walking from the bar stopped and stared across at her.'

'Maybe he knew her?' Alex said.

'She said she didn't recognise *him*, so she was doubtful he recognised *her*. It spooked her, anyway. So as soon as the dog dropped troo, they were back on the boat where she locked the door and kept the frying pan by her side. If the guy somehow got on board, she could either fry him up a couple of eggs in the morning or batter him over the napper with it, depending on what his likely intentions were. Her words, not mine.'

'Anything else?' Alex asked, hoping the coffee houseboat owner had the kettle on, or whatever else it was he used to brew coffee.

'There was nobody on the boat in front of hers. This is where it gets interesting; a young woman lives on the boat in front of that one, on her own. She heard the scream. She went up on the... whatever the top of the boat is called.'

Harry looked to Alex to see if she had the answer, but she was as clueless as he was.

'Anyway,' Gregg continued, 'she had already been heading up there for a smoke. Around midnight, the last one before she went to bed. She heard the scream and looked over here and saw a man and woman struggling.'

'Did she call us?'

'She did. And a patrol car turned out. Their report says when they got here, there was nothing.'

'If he was attacking her, then he could have stabbed her to death and shoved her over the side by the time the car got here. Nothing to do with their response times, but I'm assuming he wouldn't want to hang about,' Alex said. 'Make sure we get the report from last night and we'll want to talk to the responding officers.'

'I already got their names. They're back on duty this afternoon.'

'And they saw nobody running away, covered in blood, waving a knife?' Harry said.

'Correct. DI Shiels has been organising the door-to-door at those flats, and the other ones over there, which are serviced apartments. And the other boats moored outside those apartments on the other side of the Leamington bridge.'

'Get uniforms looking for any place that might have CCTV.'

'Will do.' Gregg walked away to join a group of uniforms.

Angie Patterson and a young Polish woman, whose

name Harry forgot but who went by the moniker *Sticks* because she played drums in a band, were loading the deceased woman into the back of their van.

'Could you stare any harder?' Alex said.

Harry turned his head towards her. 'You do realise I'm thinking of putting your name forward for re-training at Tulliallan, don't you? I mean, I can open up my email when I get to the office and hit *send*, or you can get me a coffee. That might take my mind off it.' He nodded to the houseboat coffee shop. 'Hurry up, there's a queue forming.'

'This is blackmail.'

'Black email. I like the sound of that. No milk and no sugar, if you insist on buying.'

'Only if it's your round in the pub tonight.'

'I can't make it tonight.'

'You're otherwise engaged with Angie.'

'First of all, please don't use the word *engaged*, and secondly, I'm having dinner with Vanessa.'

The smile dropped from Alex's face. 'What? Harry, no, tell me you're winding me up.'

'Her idea, not mine.'

'The way she's treated you these past few months?'

'There are two more people in line. If you don't hurry, the queue will be snaking back to the old bingo hall on Fountainbridge.'

Alex walked away, taking change out of her pocket.

'Make mine...' Gregg started to say as she passed him, but stopped when she gave him the kind of hand signal that she hadn't been taught in the Girl Guides. 'Never mind, I wasn't thirsty anyway.'

Karen Shiels walked quickly up to Harry. 'Control got back with the information on our victim. Linda Smith is dead.'

'I know, I just saw her in the forensics tent.'

'No, I mean, she was already dead.'

THREE

'A BMW isn't my first choice,' Harry admitted, 'but I do like these bum warmers.'

'Your poor wee CR-V not got the heated seats then?' Alex said, driving along Slateford Road.

'First of all, like I even need to remind you, the car is my ex-wife's.'

'Still going with that story, eh?'

He held up a hand. 'And my car is in the garage waiting for parts.'

She threw him a quick look. 'What sort of garage keeps your car for six months waiting for parts?'

'One that has dedicated craftsmen working in it, not like the robots that clearly service your overpriced jalopy.'

Alex laughed. 'Tell that to Angie. She drove it down from Dornoch for me and loved every minute.'

'Does she have her own car now?'

'Why? So she can chauffeur you about on your date?'

'We sometimes have a drink. As colleagues.'

'For your information, she doesn't have a car but uses Uber when she goes out with her older colleagues for drinks. Otherwise, she has a bus pass.'

'Good to know.'

'You'll have to dust off your Honda if you want to be a gentleman when you go out for a date. It wouldn't be the same trying to bag off with her on the back seat of a bus.'

'Your attempts at trying to get a rise out of me are sad and pathetic.' He lowered the seat heating level.

'To be honest, I'm more worried about you going out with Vanessa.'

'Why? It's a Friday night. Plenty of people go out for a meal on a Friday night.'

'*Couples*, Harry. You haven't been a couple for months now.' She turned up Craiglockhart Avenue and turned right. The address they were looking for was along on the right-hand side. A detached bungalow with a red tiled roof.

The BMW fit right into the neighbourhood.

A man answered the door and Harry played the *guess what age he is* game. Around sixty, fifty-eight if he was being kind and the man had been clean shaven.

He was leaning on a walking stick with a fancy duck's head, Harry noticed.

'Brian Smith?' Harry said as they showed their warrant cards.

'Yes.'

'Can we come in and have a word?'

'What about?'

'Linda.'

He looked unsure for a moment, as if wondering if he'd locked up the family silver, then he stepped to one side.

The house had been well kept at one time, but the discarded newspapers, dirty coffee mugs still on the coffee table, and the general air of uncleanliness told them that housework wasn't at the top of Smith's to-do list.

'Grab a seat,' he said, walking over to the little mantelpiece where he picked up a pack of cigarettes and lit one. 'I'd offer you a coffee, but I'm a lazy bastard and there's nobody else to do it, so this might not be your lucky day if you were expecting one.'

'It's fine,' Alex said, moving some magazines to sit on the couch. There was a little leather pouch on top and Smith moved to take it from her and put it on the mantelpiece. Harry looked at the only chair that didn't have its surface covered and Smith moved to it as if he'd seen Harry eying it up. Harry stood.

'What do you want to know about Linda?' Smith said, blowing out more smoke and putting his walking stick to one side, where it promptly fell on to the floor. 'I take it you know she's dead?'

'Yes, we do,' Harry said, 'and we're sorry for your loss.'

'Why? Did you know her?'

'No, we didn't.'

'Then why are you sorry?'

Alex sat up straighter. 'It's what people say, Mr Smith, out of respect.'

Smith shrugged like he couldn't care less. 'Carry on then.'

'When did she die?' Harry said.

'Three months ago. But you don't need me to tell you that. And since she was a copper, you'll know that fucker ran her down, and he was never caught. I'd have hanged the bastard, if I could. But he was never caught. You shower of bastards couldn't tie your fucking shoelaces without watching a YouTube video on how to do it.'

'We found a woman this morning, deceased, and she was carrying Linda's warrant card. Can you tell us how that came about?'

'How should I know?'

Harry gritted his teeth for a second. 'Listen, we have a dead woman who we're trying to identify, and she was carrying your daughter's warrant card, and if you could stop being a smartarse for a second and explain, then maybe we can go to the family and tell them they've just lost a daughter, much like the respect you were afforded.'

Smith looked at him for a second, as if he was about to come back with something, but then his shoulders slumped and all the wind left his sails. His lip trembled. 'I miss her. Every single day. Every single fucking day, and that scumbag is still walking God's earth. Tell me how that's fair.'

'It's not fair, Mr Smith. But it's not going to bring Linda back. She was a police officer and a good one from what I heard. We just need to know the circumstances which led up to her warrant card being on a civilian.'

Smith hung his head for a moment and his eyes were red when he looked up. 'Linda left her uniform in a holdall in her car one day. She was meeting a friend for lunch and when she came back, the window had been smashed and the uniform gone.'

'Where did this happen?'

'In the Ocean Terminal car park.'

'The fact that a uniform was stolen is a big deal. What did my colleagues do about it?'

'They checked the CCTV and saw a man with a hoodie on breaking in. He took her bag and walked out.

They tracked him all the way out into the street and then he was lost. They think he got into a car that was waiting for him.' He took a deep breath and blew it out. 'I told her not to leave stuff in sight. Especially her bloody uniform in a bag. As soon as those dirtbags see something in a car, they'll break in and steal it.'

'How long before she was killed did this happen?' Alex said.

Smith looked at her for a moment, and she could almost see the wheels in his head going round.

'Only a couple of months.'

'I'll have a look at the report later.' Harry looked at Alex, about to give her the nod to start taking some notes but she was ahead of him.

'You'll have to excuse us, Mr Smith, but my colleague and I were seconded to another force area when Linda died, so we only briefly heard about it later. Can you tell us what you were told about her death?'

'She told me she was on duty, some overtime thing. She didn't call anything in, but witnesses said they saw her lying in the road and a van driving away up the street without lights on. Maybe he'd been drinking or something and she was trying to stop him. We'll never know. The guy mowed her down and took off. He didn't stop and they found the van abandoned. It had been stolen.'

'Did she live here at home?'

'She did, but she spent a lot of time at her friend's flat down by the canal.'

Harry didn't take his eyes off the man. 'Can you tell us her name?'

'Fiona Carlton. Nice girl. I met her once, briefly, but I don't know much about her.'

'You wouldn't have an address for her, would you?'

'It was one of those new places at Lochrin Basin. Some of the flats are serviced apartments. Fountain Court they call it. I have it on my phone. Linda spent a lot of time there, so I wanted the address, you know, just for emergencies.'

He fished his phone out of his pocket and, like a lot of the older generation, took some time to find the details. 'Lower Gilmore Bank.' He gave them the number.

'Thank you, Mr Smith,' Harry said, and Alex stood up.

Outside, the wind had picked up. 'Does that thing have remote start?' Harry said, pulling his collar up.

'*Thing?* No, Betty does not have a remote start. Do you want me to ruin the environment by running the car unnecessarily?'

'I hardly think you'd be doing it single-handedly.'

They got in and there was a semblance of warmth from before.

'What do you make of Smith?' Harry asked, as Alex pulled away.

'Poor sod. I can't even imagine losing a child. What about you?'

'I can't blame him for still grieving. I'd be a basket case if something happened to my son.' Chance was Harry's only child, and he only got to see his son every so often.

She took a right and headed up towards Colinton Road, making her way back down to Viewforth. There was still a hive of activity down by the basin as Alex parked her car on Lower Gilmore Place.

Harry called Karen Shiels. Asked her if the address they were looking for had been included in the door-to-door. Uniforms were there, but hadn't reached that number yet.

They walked along the path on the canal's edge, through a communal garden to the stair door. They buzzed the number they were looking for.

'There's no guarantee she'll be in,' Alex said, just before the voice cracked through the little metal box and answered.

'Hello?'

'Police. We're looking for Fiona Carlton.'

Hesitation for a moment before the lock on the door clicked. They walked into the communal hallway and saw a young woman standing at an open door.

'Fiona?' Alex said.

'No, I'm her flatmate, Bea.' She stepped aside to let them in, then closed the door and showed them through to the living room. It was a modern apartment and with contemporary architecture came contemporary room sizes. It didn't appear that Bea had a cat, but if she did, Harry wouldn't have attempted to swing it.

A kitchen was off to one side, in a large nook.

'Coffee?' she asked. She looked like a student, dressed in old jeans and a big comfortable cardigan, and she had tucked her hands up into the sleeves.

'No thanks,' he replied and Bea indicated for them to sit down. A TV hung on what looked like a slab of wood that had been nailed to the wall, but was probably put there as a design feature. Three windows looked out onto the courtyard at the front, the bottom panes made of frosted glass. Handy if the pervert was on his hands and knees trying to peek in, but if he was feeling adventurous, he could always stand up and look through the top half of the windows.

'What's this about?' Bea asked, pulling the cardigan tighter. She yawned. 'Sorry. I was up late working last night. Sometimes I do some work from home.'

'The body of a young female was found in the canal this morning, just along from here, and she had a warrant card on her that didn't belong to her. No other identification, just the warrant card so we're trying to find out who she was.'

'Oh God, no.'

Bea jumped up out of her seat and left the living room. Harry stood up, not wanting to be caught out if Bea turned out to be an axe murderer. Alex sat on the edge of the settee, quite happy for Harry to be the cannon fodder should things take a downswing. Harry picked up a photo in a frame that had been sitting on a shelf.

Bea came rushing back in. 'Fiona's bed's not been slept in.'

'Is that Fiona?' he asked, turning back to look at Bea.

'Please don't tell me that's who you found in the canal.'

'It's somebody fitting that description. Is there any way you could try and call her?' He put the photo back.

Bea took her mobile phone out of her cardigan pocket. Harry was amazed that the phone was in there. He was old enough to remember an age without mobile phones, and the world had revolved quite happily without everybody taking photos of themselves and feeling the need to take medication when a total stranger didn't like them. It would be like him walking through a mall with a packet of photos and showing them to every Tom, Dick and Harry and having to check himself into rehab when young women told him to fuck off.

You sound like your own father, Harry, he thought, glad he hadn't voiced that opinion to Alex, who probably posted photos of her cat to Instagram every day. If she had a cat.

Bea paced the room, her mobile pressed to her left ear. 'Fee? It's Bea. Call me as soon as you get this.'

Fee and Bea, Harry thought. There had to be a punchline there somewhere.

She hung up and looked at him. 'Voicemail,' she said unnecessarily.

'Can I take one of the photos?' Alex asked.

Bea put her phone away and took one of the photos of Fee out of a frame and handed it over.

'When did you last see Fiona?' Harry asked. They were all standing in the middle of the living room now, all signs of bonne homme gone.

'Last night. She was going out for a drink or something.'

'Do you know who with?'

Bea shook her head. 'No, sorry.'

'Where does she work?'

'McCallum Technology. It's a research and development company near Bilston. I work for them too.'

'What does she do there?'

'She's a software engineer.'

'Obviously, the young woman we pulled out of the canal has similar looks to your friend, but it's not a certainty, so we would ask you to say nothing at the moment. In case we get an identification, would you know if she has a next of kin?'

Bea lowered her head for a moment, either racking her brains or she'd noticed a spot on the carpet that would need taking care of with the hoover.

'She has a sister,' she finally said, making eye contact again. 'Maggie.'

'Same last name?'

'Yes.' The phone came out again, and a finger moved across the screen with deft precision. Then she held it out for Harry to see. He put the number in his own phone, with some accuracy if not the same speed.

'Thank you. I'd also ask you to not make contact with her at the moment.'

Bea nodded. 'I understand.'

'I don't suppose you heard anything last night? Late, around midnight,' Alex asked.

Bea shook her head. 'No, sorry. I had headphones in, listening to music. I was in my room working. I'm a software engineer too. Fee and I met at uni. I wouldn't have heard Fee coming in because she knows not to disturb me when I'm working from home. We both do, at times, so we know what it's like.'

27

'Thanks anyway.'

Harry led the way out and Bea closed the door softly behind them.

'It's her, isn't it?' Alex said.

'Pound to a penny.'

FOUR

Alex drove through Bruntsfield, heading south, past Hillend and continuing on the A702.

'You ever been on the ski slope?' Alex asked him as they drove past it.

'I can think of easier ways to break my neck. And they all involve alcohol.'

'Fair do's.'

'How about you?'

'I know I'm a lean fighting machine, but like you, I prefer to keep all my limbs intact.'

Harry laughed. 'You know where you're going?'

'Do I look like I know where I'm going? That's why I bring you along.'

'No, you bring me along because I'm your boss.'

'That as well.'

Harry was holding his phone and he looked down

at the map on the screen. 'Turn left up ahead. Bush Loan Road.'

She saw the green and white sign pointing the way to Roslin, and turned left where two terraced cottages sat at the junction.

Further along the road, they turned right into the Bush Estate. A large gatehouse sat just inside the property and some new-looking low buildings were on their right. They drove past and stopped at a road on their left that had a sign at the junction. They took the left and followed it round until the magnificence that was Bush House appeared on their right.

'Can you imagine having all of this as your own property, way back when?' Alex said, impressed with the sand coloured building. They parked beside some expensive cars out the front in the little parking area.

Harry glanced around at the grounds as he stretched. It looked like a park in front of him, and if he had just opened his eyes without seeing where they had driven in, he would swear that's what it was. The sun was out, weak and watery, and the openness let a wind blow through.

A magnificent portico entrance protruded from the front of the building. Inside was a stark contrast to the outside. It was every bit as modern as the name suggested; McCallum Technology.

Inside the entrance hall, they were faced with a

wall of wood and glass. A man sat behind one of the glass panels.

'Can I help you?' he asked, his voice coming through a loudspeaker.

'Police. We're looking for somebody who works here.' He and Alex showed their warrant cards.

The man looked at them like a teller might wait for a man with sunglasses to produce a shotgun.

'Pass me your ID, please.' A metal drawer came out and he looked at them.

They put their cards in and the drawer snapped shut. The security officer took the cards and copied them before making them reappear in the drawer like he was a magician.

'Who are you looking for?'

'Maggie Carlton.'

The man typed something into a keyboard. 'Come through the door on your left. You'll be escorted to talk to somebody through there.'

A door in the wall clicked and opened by itself and a machine was waiting for them. It had a base but its body was skinny, taller than Harry. It had a dark glass screen on its face.

'Follow me, please,' it said. The skinny part turned three sixty on its base and off it went.

'There's no obvious way it's moving,' Harry said.

'Wheels?' Alex said. 'Like a hovercraft? Tracks?'

'Black magic?'

They came to another door along a short corridor and the machine stood looking at a scanner. The door opened and the machine moved through, the detectives following.

'Wait here,' it said to them, and its top half moved round again and it went back the way it had come, the door closing behind it. The door in front of them opened and they walked through and were greeted by a smiling woman behind a desk.

'Hello. I believe you're looking for Maggie Carlton?'

'Yes, we are,' Harry said. The walls were white, like a hospital. Another glass wall was blocking their entrance into the building proper, and he watched as people walked about with papers in their hands. Working or skiving? he thought.

'I'll have to call her supervisor and see if she can be taken from her work station.'

'We're not here with good news. We have to talk to her.'

'You heard the man!' a voice from their right said. A man in an electric wheelchair came around the corner, followed by another man.

'Yes, sir,' the woman said, her cheeks going slightly red, despite the man's beaming smile.

'James McCallum,' he said, holding out a hand.

'DCI Harry McNeil. DS Maxwell.' They both shook McCallum's hand.

'I got a notice through the intranet about the police being here, and I was worried you'd had a tip-off about my stash of weed.'

'No, we'll leave that for the drug squad,' Harry said.

McCallum looked to be no older than late thirties. He laughed, showing a good set of teeth. 'This is my assistant, Max Blue.' He smiled up at the man who was standing next to him.

'Pleased to meet you,' the man said, revealing his American accent.

McCallum laughed. 'Max has been my assistant ever since, well, you know...' He patted one of his legs. 'But let's go and find the young Miss Carlton.' He turned and they went through another glass door.

'What do you know about my company, detective?' McCallum asked them as he moved his wheelchair along a pristine corridor.

'Not a lot.'

'We were featured in *Techno Science* magazine last year.'

'I'm more of a *Top Gear* man myself.'

McCallum laughed. 'I do like my cars, I must say, but this is how I ended up in this contraption; too fast and overconfident.' Blue stopped at a panel next to another door, this one a sliding steel one. A reader scanned his right eye and the door slid open.

'I can talk about some of the things we do here, as they were mentioned in the magazine, but there are other things that I'm not at liberty to discuss. I hope you understand?' he said as the door slid closed behind them.

'Of course.' Harry gave Alex a couldn't-care-less look.

'Primarily, we work on AI here, and our main focus at the moment is self-driving cars. We're developing not only software but the hardware to go with it. I like to think we're ahead of the Americans at this game. They've had some disasters.'

'It can't be easy.'

They went into a lift and took it up to the next level. 'You're right, it's not. But we have some brilliant minds working for us. And since I bought Bush House, we've had some extensive work done. Did you see the new lab out front?'

Harry shook his head. 'I only saw grass and trees.'

'That's because we opened the grounds up and built an underground lab. We're doing a lot of construction here in the grounds. A lot of it has been completed and it's ongoing. We've just completed a test track for the final phase of our car testing. The world is moving along fast, Chief Inspector, and we are going to be at the forefront.'

'When I was a boy, I thought we'd be flying in cars by now.'

McCallum stopped outside an office door and smiled. 'Autonomous cars are the future, and the future is already here. Miss Carlton is waiting for you in there. If we don't get to meet again, it was nice having a brief chat. My security team will see you out.'

He moved his wheelchair along and Max Blue smiled at Alex as he walked alongside his boss.

They entered the room and a young woman was sitting on the other side of a table.

'Miss Carlton?' Harry said.

'Yes. What's wrong?'

Harry did the introductions again. 'You have a sister called Fiona?' he said as they sat down.

'Yes. Why? Has something happened?'

Harry took out his phone. 'I'm sorry to say, but a woman's body was found this morning, and we have reason to believe she may be your sister. Would you mind taking a look at a photo?'

Maggie's lips trembled, and she shook her head that she wouldn't mind.

'Oh God. That looks like her,' she said, putting a hand to her mouth.

'We're sorry to do this, but could you come with us to the mortuary for an identification?' Alex asked.

Maggie started crying. Alex got up and went round to her, putting a hand on her shoulder.

'I know this must be hard, but we'll make it as quick as possible.'

After a few minutes, she brought her head up. 'I'll go and get my things together.'

'We can drive you if you don't feel up to it.'

'No, I'll take my car.'

She left the room and the two detectives followed, waiting in the corridor.

They waited five minutes. Then ten. When fifteen minutes passed, Harry started getting antsy. 'Where has she got to?'

A door opened in the wall facing them, the one that Maggie Carlton had just gone through. A woman appeared, letting the door close behind her.

'We're waiting for Miss Carlton,' Harry said as she looked at them.

'She's not here.'

'What do you mean? She was here a few minutes ago.'

'I mean she just left. Maggie Carlton is no longer on the premises.'

FIVE

'I've never had that before,' Alex said as she backed her car out of the parking space. 'I imagine you have though; having a woman leave without any explanation.'

'I've had some rough dates, I admit. But they all soldiered on to dessert.'

As Alex drove through the south of the city heading for Maggie Carlton's address, Harry made use of the time to call DI Karen Shiels.

'Tell me you've found the culprit, preferably covered in blood with some sort of sharp object on his person.'

'We're still working on that, sir. We've called the dive team in to search the canal, in case he threw the weapon in there.'

'How are we on the witnesses?'

'Nothing else reported.'

He explained where they were heading and hung up.

The address they had been given was in Baberton Mains on the west of the city, just off the city bypass. Alex drove round the main road until they found the side street they were looking for.

'Down on the right,' Harry said.

They had been told what kind of car she drove as well as her address and Harry spotted it in a little cul-de-sac off the road. A green Volkswagen Beetle. The house was detached with a garage way in the back of the garden.

They saw a plume of smoke coming from the back garden and Harry walked up the driveway. It was damp and cold but the property was shielded by trees on one side. Alex was just behind him.

They looked over the small, wrought iron gate and saw Maggie Carlton standing throwing papers into a box that had flames licking out of it.

'Mind if we come in and warm our hands?' he said.

'Not at all,' Maggie replied. 'I was expecting you.'

Harry opened the gate and they walked through and across to her. 'Early bonfire?'

She looked at him. 'It's not illegal to do this.'

'I didn't say it was.' He could feel the heat from the fire as the wind blew the flames around. There was a small bottle of white spirit and a watering can nearby. One to kick start it, the other to put it out, but the watering can wouldn't do much good if some embers flew onto the house and set it on fire.

'If you were expecting us, then you'll know what my first question is going to be.'

She looked at him, took one of the papers from the top of the pile, scrunched it and threw it into the flames. 'It's not as if I don't want to go to the mortuary with you.'

'But...?' Alex said.

More papers into the fire. Harry noticed a box at her feet with more in it.

'But, I needed to come home and do this. Besides, if you weren't aware, they were listening to us.'

'How do you know that?' Alex asked.

'After I said I would get my coat, there were two security guards waiting in the lift, weren't there?'

'They could have been waiting there before we went into that room.'

'And the moon is made of cheese.' More papers, more flames.

'We'd still like you to come to the mortuary with us, if you don't mind. Unless your parents are alive and we could ask either one of them?'

She snapped her head at them. 'No. They're both dead.' Another few sheets went to meet their maker.

'Fiona left a lot of stuff behind when she moved into the apartment. It's no use to me now.'

Harry looked down and saw a newspaper clipping before Maggie grabbed it, balled it up and threw it into the fire.

It was a story about a helicopter crash.

SIX

They stood around in the little waiting room across from the viewing area, like they were actors in a horror movie. Harry had spent four years investigating other police officers and was a little out of the loop, despite being back on regular duties for a few months. Alex, on the other hand looked like this was second nature to her. Which it wasn't as she had spent a lot of time working in the cold case unit.

'I'll be right here with you, Maggie,' she said, putting a hand on the other woman's arm.

'Thank you, Alex.'

Harry turned round when Angie Patterson, one of the mortuary assistants, approached the entrance. He started a little bit but shrugged as if he was only adjusting his overcoat without using his hands.

'They're ready for you, sir,' she said.

He nodded and turned back to Maggie. 'If you could approach the glass now, Miss Carlton. Take your time.'

She walked out of the little room, followed by Alex and walked up to the window. Harry stood back, watching. When Maggie was ready, Angie gently knocked on the glass window and the curtains behind it rolled to the sides, revealing the body with a sheet covering her.

One of the other attendants, Sticks, real name Natalie, Harry now remembered, was standing to one side. Maggie stepped closer to the glass and looked down at the woman's face, freshly cleaned, her hair in a style that wasn't how the woman would have worn it in life.

'That's my sister, Fiona,' Maggie said, and then the tears came. She stepped away from the glass and Angie nodded to Sticks who closed the curtain.

'Thank you,' Harry said to Angie, who merely nodded, then she stopped as she was about to walk away.

'Sorry, I forgot to say that Kate Murphy wants a word, sir.'

He turned to Alex. 'I'll be out in a minute, if you want to wait in the car.'

'Okay.'

'You're enjoying all this *sir* stuff, aren't you?' Angie said as they walked down the corridor to the offices.

'I am indeed.'

They walked through a set of rubber doors. 'I haven't seen you in the pub for a little while,' she said.

'I haven't been to be honest. We'll have to do a catch-up sesh soon. Just the four of us.'

'I'll look forward to it.'

'How's the flat hunting going?'

'It's steady. I haven't found anywhere I want to settle down yet. The rented place is okay.'

'I'll keep my ears open.'

Doctor Kate Murphy was in her office. A detective from one of the other Major Investigation Teams was there, a man who Harry had worked a case with just a few months ago.

'Sorry to disturb,' Harry said, knocking on the door.

DS Andy Watt was sitting on the edge of the desk and stood up when Harry came in. 'I was just leaving, sir,' Watt said.

'No need, Andy. Kate said she wanted a word.'

Watt stood to one side while Kate picked up a clear plastic bag that was sitting on her desk. 'This was in Fiona Carlton's shoe.'

Harry took the bag and looked inside. 'A flash drive. Funny place to keep it. Do you know what's on it?'

'We just bagged it. That's for your computer geeks to figure out.'

'Oh, I'm sure they would appreciate being called that,' Watt said.

'I'm sure they've been called worse, Andy,' Harry said. 'Besides, it gives them validation, otherwise we'd be thinking of them as amateurs. I'll pass it on to them.'

'Okay. DI Shiels was here for the preliminary exam but we'll do the full autopsy tomorrow. I've been run off my feet.'

'Okay. Talk to you soon. Good seeing you again, Andy.'

'You too, sir.'

Outside, the late afternoon cold was starting to grip the city.

'I'm sorry for your loss,' Harry said. 'It's never an easy thing, coming to the mortuary.'

'I appreciate that. Would you mind driving me to my sister's flat before taking me home? She had borrowed a laptop from me. I'd like it back.'

'Not at all.'

Alex drove them up to Lochrin and parked in the underground car park.

They rang the buzzer on the front door but there was no answer. 'I have a key,' Maggie said. She let them in.

They walked into the living room but Bea wasn't

there. 'Maybe she's in bed. I just wanted to look at my sister's stuff.'

Maggie walked into Fiona's bedroom and stopped.

'What's wrong?' Harry said.

'This room. It's spotless.'

'Is there a problem?' Alex asked, looking around the room at the bed that was made, at the dresser that was tidy and the small desk that was neat.

Maggie turned to her. 'Yes, yes, it is. My sister wasn't a slob, but she would have clothes lying about. She would catch up with laundry at the weekend. But look.' She stepped forward to the small dresser. Ran a finger across the top. 'There's not a speck of dust on here. Like it's brand new and not even had time to collect dust yet.'

She walked over to the laptop sitting on the desk. It was open. She pressed the on button and the computer came to life moments later.

Maggie stepped back like she'd just stepped on a Lego brick.

'Somebody's touched this.'

'How do you know?' Harry said, stepping forward and looking at the screen. It had one of Apple's wallpapers on it.

'First of all, she had a photo of me and her on here as background. And secondly, she wouldn't have put a default photo up.' She leaned over and started clicking the keys.

'Christ, there are no documents on here.' She straightened up and looked at them. 'I mean, we don't leave important stuff on these machines, in case they get stolen, but there is generic work done here that we can email to the supervisors. Then it's all deleted. There's nothing here.'

She went back and clicked again. 'Jesus, there's not even any of my photos here.' She straightened again.

'What's going on?' a voice said from the doorway.

They all turned to see Bea standing there.

'We're just looking at Fiona's laptop.'

'Oh, okay.' Bea looked at Harry. 'This is a secure serviced apartment for employees of McCallum Technology only. They don't allow non-staff in here, for confidentiality purposes.'

'I am a police officer,' he said, not appreciating her tone. 'And we're here for personal belongings. I'm sure Mr McCallum wouldn't mind, and if he does, then he can call me directly.'

Bea shrugged. 'No, it's fine. I just know how strict they are about having people in here.'

'We'll take it away and have it examined,' Alex said. 'In case there's any deleted stuff we can't get into.'

'I can look, if you like.'

Harry held up a hand. 'We're taking it in for our tech people to have a look at it.'

'Okay, no problem.' She walked away and into the kitchen.

'Anything seem to be missing?' Alex said in low voice.

Maggie scoured the room. 'Nothing jumps out at me.'

'Have you got an evidence bag on you?' Alex asked. 'I'll take this home and have the tech guys look at it first thing tomorrow morning.'

Harry pulled one out of his pocket. Just like the nitrile gloves, you never knew when you were going to need it.

'I'm going to stay here for a little while. I want to look through some of Fiona's things. I want to still feel connected to her. Even though...' Her voice trailed off.

'I can't let you do that. I'm going to call forensics to come round here and look through her things. I hope you understand,' Harry said.

Maggie nodded, while Alex went to tell Bea not to enter the bedroom.

Half an hour later, the crew turned up and went to work.

SEVEN

It was dark and cold. Just what Harry's ex-girlfriend had called him not that long ago.

'How does my tie look?' he asked Alex. He was FaceTiming her from his living room.

'It won't win any competitions, but I think it's perfect for tonight.'

'You mean, it'll do just for seeing Vanessa?'

'Exactly.' She smiled and took a sip of the wine she was drinking. She too was at home. 'Chin-chin.'

'She just wants to have a quiet chat,' he said in his own defence.

'Harry, she lives just across the road from you.'

'Along the road and round the corner, to be precise.'

'You can see her house from your window if you look right across the bowling green.'

'Okay, now we've established where Vanessa lives, can we move on?'

He carried the phone in front of him, moving from the bathroom mirror into the living room.

'My point is, she could have walked round to your flat, or vice versa. Just be careful you're not walking into a trap.'

'It's hardly the gunfight at the O.K. Corral.' Although he'd seen many a fight in Edinburgh that wasn't far off it.

'I'm just saying. I know I've only ever met her the one time, when we were all in the pub and she waltzed in with some of her staff, but I just sized her up right away. I could see she took an instant dislike to me.'

'I think you're imagining it, Alex.'

'You're not a woman. You wouldn't understand.'

'It's just a meal and a drink. As friends.'

'Okay. If you say so.'

'I do. And thanks for your help.'

'Catch you tomorrow. Oh, look at the time. Me and Angie Patterson are having a couple tonight in Diamonds bar.'

'Have fun.'

'You too.'

He signed off, feeling a knot in his guts. Why wouldn't Vanessa like Alex? He knew you couldn't make somebody like you, but Alex was likeable. He

put his jacket on just as he heard the car horn
downstairs.

'Have you ever been here before?' Vanessa asked as the
taxi dropped them off outside Gusto's, an Italian
restaurant in George Street.

He had thought they knew everything there was to
know about each other when they had been dating, but
maybe in the few months they'd been apart, she had
wiped her mental hard drive clean.

'No. You?'

She gave him a sly look, one his mother used to use
when he'd got caught taking a biscuit from the tin
when he was a boy. *You should know that, Harry,* she
was saying, and didn't bother replying.

Harry paid the taxi and dodged through a small group
of women who looked like they were bar hopping. Friday
night in the centre of Edinburgh. It had been a long time.
He remembered the shifts he'd done here when he had
been in uniform. It went like a fair until the wee hours.

'You coming or what?' Vanessa said, the smile on
her face belying the aggravation in her voice.

He strode forward and they went into the warmth
of the place. Harry liked Italian and had suggested it to

Vanessa, like he knew the place. Truth was, Alex had given him the tip about it.

They made chit-chat while they ordered their food, a pizza for Harry and Vanessa had salmon fillet with saffron potatoes.

'How are you liking being the boss of an MIT?' she said after ordering some wine.

'It's good. It's what I was used to, being in CID before going to Professional Standards.'

'Alex seems nice.' She looked at him over the rim of the glass that had been tipped up to her mouth.

'She is. She's a good detective and she'll go far. She'll be my boss one day, no doubt.'

'Among other things.'

'What's that supposed to mean?' He took a sip from the bottle of beer.

Vanessa grinned. 'She fancies you.'

'What? Behave.'

'She does, Harry. I'm a woman. We see things that men can't.'

'Listen, when you're a cop, you become close to other cops you work with. I'm close to Karen Shiels, too.'

'No you're not. Not like Alex.'

'You're being ridiculous.'

'Am I?' There was something in her eyes now as

the waiter brought their order. Harry felt a heat inside, fuelled by anger.

'We're colleagues, nothing more. You know how it was with me in Standards; all my old friends wanted nothing more to do with me. It's hard trying to work with people who don't trust you, but luckily, I'm working with people now who do trust me. Yes, Alex and I get on better than I'd hoped, and we have a bit of a laugh, and we go out for a drink with some of our other colleagues. But that's where I draw the line.'

He could feel his face flush as he cut into his pizza. Christ, it was like being in an interview room back at the station.

'Don't get all defensive on me now.' She smiled at him. She had gone into a battle of wits with him and won. He mentally kicked himself.

'I'm not getting defensive, I'm just telling you how it is. Why should you worry now?'

'I'm not worried. In fact, I couldn't be less worried. I just asked you to dinner so we could have a civilised chat. So I could tell you my news.'

He finished his bottle of beer and asked the waiter for another one.

'Go on then, I'll take the bait; what news?'

'I've moved on, Harry. These past few months have been hell. I've lost weight...'

He looked at her, struggling to see the difference, an opinion he would keep to himself for the moment.

'I've not been sleeping well. I even contemplated doing something stupid at one time.'

Something stupid probably meant doing a prank call on him in the middle of the night. There were people out there who really did contemplate doing something stupid, and now she was comparing herself to them. He couldn't be more disgusted.

'Let's not forget something here, Vanessa; you chose this. You made the choice to call it a day.'

'Just because you backed me into a corner.'

'By not giving up the lease on my flat? Christ, we were doing fine. Everything was ticking along nicely, until you wanted me to – *step into your lair* – move in with you.'

'People do that sort of thing. Move in with each other.'

'I'm sorry, I didn't feel comfortable doing that. Not last summer.'

'And now?'

The waiter brought the bottle and Harry drank from it, all thoughts of his pizza now gone.

'You called it a day. What else do you want me to say?'

'I met somebody, Harry. One of the fathers who

has a little boy in my nursery. His wife left him, we got talking and he asked me out. I said yes.'

'Why are you here with me then, and not him?'

'I'm meeting him later. I just wanted to tell you about him here.'

'In a public place, in case I had a meltdown? You don't have to worry about that.'

She was looking down at her phone, her thumbs dancing across the screen. 'Work,' she said, looking back at him and smiling. 'Listen, I don't want this to end awkwardly. I want us to stop in the street and say hi if we bump into each other. Especially since we live around the corner from each other.'

'Fine. We can stop and talk about the weather. How does that sound?'

Her phone buzzed just then. She picked it up and again her thumbs were dancing. 'Harry, I'm so sorry. I have to go.'

There it was; the get out of Dodge routine. He called the waiter over and explained they had an emergency and he paid the bill.

Outside, it was cold and damp. Never mind, only a few days before Edinburgh set fire to itself, he thought.

'This is it, Harry. We go our separate ways.' She pecked him on the cheek before starting to walk away. Then she stopped and turned around. 'Thanks for dinner.'

The last supper. He stood at the kerb, waiting for a taxi, which wouldn't take long. He watched a man move away from the wall further along, and Vanessa walked up to him and kissed him on the cheek. Harry guessed the man had been responsible for the *Get me the hell out of here* text Vanessa had been sent.

He shook his head and put out a hand for the taxi driving towards him.

EIGHT

Vanessa could have called him and told him the news about her new boyfriend, but she had chosen to make a display of it, making sure he saw the new man in her life. He tried to brush it off but the feeling wasn't going away anywhere soon.

The taxi took him down to the St Bernard's bar in Raeburn Place, walking distance back to his flat further along in Comely Bank.

It was busy, mostly with older clients, but a few younger ones were getting fuelled up on cheaper prices before getting ready to part with their hard-earned up town.

Harry was settling in, chatting with a couple of the older blokes he knew just from coming in here, when the front door opened. He idly looked round and did a double take. It was Alex. She hadn't seen him and squeezed her way through to the bar to order a drink. He excused himself and sidled up to her.

'Can I buy a lady a drink?'

'No thanks...' she started to say but then saw who it was and smiled. 'I was about to add some derogatory comment if you didn't go away,' she said.

'That's the normal effect I have on women,' he said, getting the barman to give him a half to add to his pint.

'Glass half empty or half full?' Alex said, nodding to his glass.

'Vanessa always said I'm the half-empty type. Me? Depends on what the weather is like.'

They moved away from the bar and found a corner to stand in, then a couple vacated a table, heading for more exciting climes and they grabbed it.

'Talking of the great Vanessa, how did your date go?'

'First of all, it was not a date, as you fine well know.'

'I'm a detective, so let's examine the evidence; Friday night, both unattached, going to dinner and having a few drinks. Where I come from, that constitutes a date.'

'Where you come from, they eat their young.'

'Don't be cheeky. You know I'm right. That's why you're flushed and sweating. Or is that just because you saw me?'

'Okay, I'm bowing to your pressure here. Your interrogation skills are second to none.'

'And yet, here I am, still waiting for the juicy gossip. Will they get back together? Has Vanessa finally seen through Harry's devious ways? What does Harry say that will bring them both crashing down? Tune in to next week's episode...'

'Oh, for God's sake. She wanted to have dinner to tell me she's found somebody else. Satisfied?'

'She wanted to publicly humiliate you.'

'She also sent a text then got one back, feigning some work emergency. Then her boyfriend met her along the road.'

'The old *This date is shite, get me out of here* text. Yeah, I've used that one before.' She took her phone out of her pocket and looked at it. 'Sorry, Harry, I have to go.'

'Really. Everything okay?'

She laughed. 'See how easy it is?'

'Christ, you were convincing.'

'Like she was, I'll bet. But why not just call you and let you know? That would have been easier, but no, she wanted to flaunt it in your face. It was all staged.'

She saw him looking into his pint for a second, then put a hand on his arm. 'She was just playing a game with you. She's trying to get in your head now.'

Harry looked up at her. 'It's not working. Yes, I was pissed off, but I knew she was trying to get a rise out of me and it didn't work.'

'You're the bigger person here.'

'I know.' He drank some of his pint. 'What about you? I thought you were meeting Angie Patterson tonight?'

'We did, but she's on-call, and was only drinking some fancy French fizzy water. And try saying that three times fast.'

'It's not even ten yet, and here we are in a little boozer that's not even in the city centre, on a Friday night. I feel old.'

'You and me both, and you're a lot older than me.'

'Ten years is hardly classed as *a lot older*.'

'I'm only thirty and I feel like I should be in a nightclub somewhere, being swept off my feet.'

'Why aren't you?' Harry looked at her face, watching her closely.

'I could call up a couple of friends and go dancing with them, but I just don't feel like it anymore. My fiancé gave me trust issues. I hate to admit that, but him cheating on me has made me put my guard up.'

'You're too young to be feeling like this. There's a lonely man out there, standing with his back to the wall, looking out on the dance floor, wishing he had somebody like you to dance with. Waiting to go home to his mother if he doesn't get a pull. He won't meet you if you don't go out.'

'Ha bloody ha.'

'Seriously, there's somebody out there waiting for you.'

'That's very philosophical. Too much for Friday night. You want a chaser?'

'Sounds good. A wee nip.' He watched her go to the bar and couldn't understand why men weren't falling over her, but then, men did have a sixth sense for women who were putting up a barrier. A few minutes conversation would give them the message. He didn't blame her. He hadn't been cheated on in his own marriage – that he knew of – but he could imagine how hard it would be to find out the person you loved didn't want to give you that love and trust back.

She sat back down with the two glasses.

'Cheers,' he said and they clinked glasses.

'Don't look round, but I think there's somebody following me,' she said.

Harry suddenly went into self-protection mode. He was sitting with his back to the door.

'What's he look like?'

'Around fifty. Close-cropped hair. Big guy. Black jacket. Standing at the bar, nursing a pint but not drinking much of it.'

Harry turned slightly as the door opened and an older man entered. He smiled and waved to the man, who he didn't know, but it afforded him the opportunity to look at the man at the bar. He was clean shaven and had the look of somebody who had been round the block.

'I see him. But why do you think he's following you?'

'He was in Diamonds up the road too.'

'Call Angie, just to make sure she's okay.'

Alex took her phone out and called their friend, and Angie assured her she was already home.

'She's fine. Tucked up on the couch with her cat, watching Netflix.'

Then Harry saw the man stand up straight and nod to the barman. He left without looking in their direction.

'Maybe I was wrong,' she said.

'Probably just a guy out for a few pints.'

'Norrie nae mates.'

Neither of them completely dismissed the idea that he'd been following Alex.

Harry got up and bought a couple of drinks, waiting patiently. Then he sat back at the table. At least they could breathe. He remembered the days when this place would be like it was on fire with the cigarette smoke.

'Do you think this murder was a mugging gone wrong?' Alex asked him.

'No. It was too vicious.'

'We have a nutter on the loose, then.'

'No. I think he was looking for something. The something that was hidden in her shoe.'

'The flash drive. Why would she have a flash drive in her shoe?'

'And what's on it?'

'We won't know until the tech boys have had a look, Harry.'

'I wonder if it's any good after being in the water.'

'We'll soon find out.'

After finishing her drink, Alex looked at him. 'I'm going to hit the hay.'

'I'll walk you home,' Harry said. 'If you like.'

'Okay. But listen...'

He put a hand up. 'Just to your front door. I'm going back to my place. Just walking you to your door.'

'Let's go.'

Her flat was literally a five-minute walk from the pub, round the corner, down a narrow lane and into the first street of the Stockbridge colonies.

'Reid Terrace,' Alex said, 'named after one of the men who originally invested in the building of the colonies.'

'Funny last name for a bloke, *Terrace*.'

'You're too bloody funny at times.'

It was well lit, with a small green in front, bordering the Water of Leith. Alex lived halfway down. The doors here were all up a small set of steps, these flats being the upper ones.

'Thanks, Harry. I would invite you up for a drink, but... you know...'

'I said to your front door. I'll stay here until you get in.'

'I would have walked round myself if I hadn't met you in the pub, you know.' She laughed. 'You're very chivalrous.'

'I've been called worse.'

Two things happened almost at once; the headlight on a motorbike parked further along sprang into life as the engine kicked over, and Alex's front door burst open and a man wearing a helmet roughly pushed past her and started running down the steps.

'Hey!' she screamed.

Harry tried to grab the person, but was roughly pushed away.

The motorbike came firing along her street and the passenger jumped on. Harry saw a wheelie bin just inside the small garden next to the steps, picked it up and fired it at the bike. It caught the pillion passenger and knocked him off. The bike carried on and the passenger got up like he had just bounced off the road.

Then as the bike turned the corner and roared away, headlights from a car came into the street and stopped. Harry started running after the passenger from the bike, but he was fast. The car was a big, black Range Rover. The driver's window rolled down and Harry thought it was the man from the pub, but he couldn't be sure. The running man opened the back door and the big car shot backwards.

Harry stopped, and turned and ran back towards Alex's flat. She wasn't at the front door so he ran up the steps. Then he looked over the Water of Leith and saw the motorbike and Range Rover speeding along the road opposite.

Alex was standing outside her front door at the top of the steps.

As Harry approached he noticed the wheels on her car and pointed them out to her.

'Bastards. They've slashed my tyres!' Alex said, coming down to have a look.

'I don't see any slash marks. It looks like they just let all the air out of them.'

'Crap. That's not so bad, but it's going to take some time to blow them up.'

'They're run flats. You could drive round to a petrol station. We can have a patrol car drive behind you later, just so you get there in one piece.'

'Later. Not tonight. I might be over the limit.'

'Fair enough.'

'They went back up to the flat.'

'Did he take anything?' Harry asked as she looked around. Then she turned to him.

'He took what he came for.'

'You mean...?'

'Yes. The MacBook Pro. Unfortunately, he took the wrong one.'

'What do you mean?'

'I mean, I keep one sitting next to the stereo over there. It's knackered. It's an old one, and I bought a new one, but instead of throwing the old one out, I kept it out as a decoy. As you well know, thieves want to be in and out, and they look for laptops and iPads and the like.'

'That makes sense.'

'The one I took from Fiona Carlton's house is in the tech lab in Fettes. I told you I was going to drop it off on Monday, but you and I know it's open seven days. Two other people thought I was going to bring it home until Monday; Maggie Carlton and Bea Anderson.

'That bloke we saw in the pub who we thought was following you; I think the passenger jumped into the back of a Range Rover and baldy was driving it.'

She looked at him. 'See? I thought the bastard was following me.'

'I think whoever wanted that laptop was keeping an eye on you and reporting to the reprobates on the bike. This was no ordinary housebreaking, and they are not amateurs.'

'At least he didn't get my new laptop. That would have been a pain.'

'I'll call this in then we'll get the forensics here.'

Alex nodded and went through to the kitchen to switch the kettle on, feeling a bit shaken. What if the guy had had a knife? Would she have been able to take him?

Thank God, Harry was there.

Within five minutes, the small street was bathed in flashing blue lights. Within half an hour, the other members of Harry's team were there.

'Boss,' Simon Gregg said as he entered the living room ahead of DI Karen Shiels. There was another woman behind them.

Karen turned to look at her before addressing Harry. 'Sir, this is the newest recruit to our team, DC Evelyn Bell. She was going to join us on Monday morning, but she's a friend of mine and she was at my place when I got the call.'

Harry smiled and shook her hand. 'Welcome aboard, Evelyn,' he said. 'I've heard good things about you.'

'Thank you, sir, but you can call me Eve.'

'Eve it is.'

'What's going on here, sir?' Gregg said. The smallish room made him look like a giant.

'Somebody broke in here, looking for something. They didn't get it.' He explained about the computer and the people who had come looking for it.

'If they took the wrong one, they might come back for round two,' Gregg said. 'I'd like to meet the little bastard you knocked off the motorbike. I'd make sure he couldn't sit down for a week.'

'You do know I was in Professional Standards, don't you?' Harry said.

Gregg had the good grace to look embarrassed. 'Just words, sir. I wouldn't really kick him up the arse, much as I'd like to.'

'I understand, but somebody else took over my position, investigating cops like us. Just one word out of turn and somebody reports it and they'll be all over you. You just won't know it.'

'Sorry, sir. I was just venting. Maybe the guy will come back. Maybe he'll come at me with a knife. Then I can arrest him.'

'Trust me, son, these boys don't come at people unprepared. If they want to fuck us over, I'm sure they're well versed in it. These guys were professionals all the way.'

'You think they could be behind Fiona Carlton's murder?' Karen asked.

'It's what I was thinking. But the description we got of the man who stood and looked at the woman with the dog who lives on the houseboat, doesn't compare to the guy I saw tonight. The description she gave was of a man wearing a woollen hat and a scarf round his face. The bald guy I saw tonight made no attempt to hide himself. He was following Alex, and we saw him in the pub.'

'You both saw him in the pub?'

'We bumped into each other round the corner.' He looked at Eve. 'I live along the road in Comely Bank so the pub is one of my regular haunts.'

'You don't have to explain, sir,' Gregg said.

'I know I don't. Just breaking down the dynamics of how this went down tonight.' He looked up at Gregg, waiting for more questions to field, but none came.

'We also got a flash drive that had been stuck in the dead woman's shoe. I passed that on to the tech team at Fettes, and they said they would start working on it. I don't know how far they got, but I'll call in the morning.' He looked at Eve. 'They work seven days, in case you didn't know that. But they'll be closed just now.'

'I knew that, sir.'

'I don't think Alex should be here by herself. Things could turn out way differently next time.'

'You're right. She could crash at my place.'

Alex came into the room. 'I appreciate it, ma'am, but I won't be pushed out of my own home. If they come back, they'll have to deal with me.'

'There was a team of them,' Harry said. 'They could have more with them next time.'

A white-suited forensics man came up to them. 'We have a lot of prints, but round the door, nothing. And by that, I mean, it looks like before he came in, he wiped the door area round the lock and the door jamb. These were professionals who knew what they were doing. I doubt we'll get anything useful. Sorry to be the bearer of bad news.'

'It's nothing we weren't expecting,' Harry said.

'I'm not happy about you staying here by yourself, Alex,' Karen said.

'Okay. Then I'll go and stay with a friend,' she said, relenting. 'Maybe you're right. We don't know how dangerous they are.' She grabbed a bag from her room and came out with it.

'That was quick,' Harry said.

'It's my bug-out bag. In case the zombie apocalypse happens.'

'Good God,' Harry said, shaking his head. 'Did you remember to pack your Spiderman pyjamas?'

'It's a real thing, boss,' Gregg said. 'Millions of people all over the world are ready for it.'

'I might have guessed you would get him roped into it.'

She laughed. 'Let's just call it my weekend-away bag, then. In case you get scared of the big, bad monsters.'

'I'd be more worried about a bloody nutter in a Range Rover than the undead.'

After the forensics crew had left, they went their separate ways.

Harry accepted a lift from Karen, with Eve sitting in the back. Gregg took Alex.

'See you first thing Monday,' Harry said, getting out of Karen's car. He watched her drive away and looked up the hill towards Vanessa's house. The outside light was on, waiting for her to come home with her new boyfriend.

Things had been ticking along nicely, and it had only gone pear-shaped because he didn't want to give up his rental flat. Something stupid could turn your whole life upside down.

Upstairs, he switched the TV on and watched some mindless crap. He should have been out with Vanessa instead.

He took his phone out and thought about calling

his son, Chance, but then thought better of it as it was so late.

Then his buzzer rang from downstairs at the front door.

He picked up the intercom.

'Hello?'

'It's Alex.'

He was silent for a moment. Should he tell her to come back in the morning? Was Gregg with her? He didn't want this to turn into some sort of sesh. He'd feel obligated to crack open a bottle of Bells, just to be sociable, although Gregg was driving, so maybe he wouldn't have to. Maybe a quick coffee...

'Thank you,' he heard Alex say, her voice sounding distant now.

'Alex?' he said, speaking to himself now. No reply, and he could hear feet thumping on the stone steps. Christ, she was coming up.

He opened the door just as she got there, out of breath, holding her bag.

'I hope you don't mind. I told Simon just to drop me off at HQ. I told him I wanted to speak to somebody and I'd get an Uber.'

'You'd better come in,' he said, stepping back. 'You didn't get an Uber, did you?'

'No, I just walked.'

She came in and walked through to the living room where she dropped her bag next to the settee.

'You want something to drink?' he said.

'What you got?'

'Horlicks. Cocoa.'

'I'm fine.'

'So what happened?' He indicated for her to take a seat.

'Nothing. I went to the lab to see if they'd done anything with the computer yet. They're already closed for the day. It's got me wound up, somebody being in my home.'

Alex stood up. 'Right, I'm going home. I'll call you tomorrow.'

'What do you mean, going home? I thought you were going to stay with a friend?'

'Yeah, well, I thought she was a friend. Turns out, not quite so much. It was a definite *no* to my sleeping on her couch.'

'Jesus.'

'It's the uniform for some people. They think it changes us personally. I mean, I've been out having a drink with her, just a couple of months ago. It doesn't matter though; I'll jam a chair behind the front door.'

Harry had a feeling that a chair would be nowhere near enough to keep the men out.

He stood up. 'I'll make up the spare bed.'

'Oh God, no. I couldn't do that.'

'Why not? There's a lock on the inside of the door. Jam a chair up against it too, if it makes you feel any better.'

'Look, boss, I don't want the others to think I'm trying to get a leg-up by... staying overnight with the boss.'

'Nobody has to know. And FYI, you're not getting a leg-up.'

She smiled. 'If you're sure we can just keep this to ourselves?'

'Trust me on that. And close the curtains will you? No point in advertising the fact.'

As Harry walked through to the linen cupboard to grab some sheets and a couple of blankets, one thought occurred to him; what if they know where I live too?

NINE

Harry thought he'd get up early and have a shower before Alex got up, but she was already in the kitchen making coffee when he eventually got dressed.

'I didn't disturb you, did I?' she said, pouring him a coffee.

'No, no, not at all.' *I always get up at seven thirty on a Saturday morning.* 'You sleep okay?'

'Eventually. I kept thinking about those guys and what's so important about that damn computer.'

'Let's go across the road and find out,' he said. 'You had breakfast?'

'No. I thought we could grab a roll in the canteen.'

'Sounds good to me.'

They made their way downstairs. It was overcast with a little wind throwing the fallen leaves about.

'You want me to drive?' she said, grinning, when Harry unlocked the CR-V.

'I do still have my faculties about me,' he said, getting in behind the wheel and starting it up.

'That's not what I meant.'

'I know what you meant, and I'm not rising up to the debate of whether or not men drive these cars.'

'There's nothing wrong with them.'

'I know,' he said, stopping at the end of the road. He took a little longer than was necessary looking up to his left. Where Vanessa's house was. Her Lexus was parked in the street.

Alex's face took on a serious note. 'She set out to play games with you and it looks like it worked,' she said. 'If Vanessa's moved on, then it's fine for you to move on too.'

'I know. I thought that van was coming right down the hill.'

'He turned two minutes ago.'

He pulled away. Alex was right; Vanessa had drawn a line under their relationship, so he had to as well. He felt like a teenager who had been dating the most popular girl in school before she moved on.

He parked in the car park at the side of the police headquarters. Their office was located in here, though there was talk of relocating them, but the big yins upstairs hadn't decided where to yet.

'Ah, it's the heid honcho,' a young technician said as they walked into the lab down on the basement level.

'You got anything yet, Ricky?' Harry said.

Ricky Morrison, young, eager, and what he didn't know about computers could be written on an ant's arse.

'I've been up since the crack of dawn.' He looked at his watch. 'Well, not the crack, you understand, but not far off it. But I digress.'

'Yes, you do,' Harry said, grabbing a tall bar stool at the side of a workbench. On the bench sat a MacBook Pro, presumably the one that the thieves were after. Alex sat on the other side of Morrison.

'Whoa, whoa, what's this? I haven't had anybody sit so close to me since fourth year and I had to stay behind and show my teacher a thing or two. But that's a story for another day.'

He grinned at them. 'I had a look at the computer when I came in first thing. I looked in the files, and in the sub-files. I was able to find a lot of technical drawings and the like. Nothing out of the ordinary, I'm afraid.'

'What sort of drawings were they?' Alex asked.

'Schematics, mostly. Electronic things. Blueprints for electrical paraphernalia.'

'Just random gobbledegook?' Harry said.

'To the untrained eye,' Morrison said. 'But to young Ricky, it's just another day at the office. These my friend, are schematics for battery-powered vehicles. Nothing too science fiction, but then I loaded the flash drive into one of our computers here, and then it all made sense.'

There was a silence for a second, a pause for dramatic effect.

'Come on, Ricky, don't keep us in suspense for God's sake,' Harry said, beginning to think the coffee in the canteen was the best thing he'd ever looked forward to, and why hadn't they gone there before coming here to see the young geek?

'There are technical drawings and code on the flash drive. They're like two pieces of a puzzle. If you take the information from the flash drive, and put it together with the schematics on the computer, the two pieces fit together. It's like if you were to draw three small squares, and you needed to add another small square to make a big square, then the fourth square is on the flash drive. Now, that's it in the simplest terms. However, there is one problem.'

'What's that?' Alex asked.

'I could tell what was missing from the schematics on the computer, and there was another schematic on the flash drive that should have worked, should have fit in to make the square. If we're still using the square analogy. But the fourth bit that's needed isn't quite a little square. It's more like an oval.'

Harry tried not to look blank, but missed the mark.

'Sorry. Let me try again. It's like drawing a car and a space for the engine. You haven't drawn the engine bay big enough. Your engine just won't go in. So you saw the corners off and shoehorn it in. It's there, it's connected and you even get it running, but it's not as silky smooth as if it would have been had you designed it the right size.'

'You're saying, there are two projects that are supposed to link up, but one of them doesn't work with the other?' Harry said.

'Bingo. By all accounts, both designs should click together, but they don't.'

Harry stood up. 'Thanks, Ricky.'

'No problem. Might see you in the police club one night. We'll get a game of darts.'

'As long as you don't want to play cards for money.'

TEN

The drive up to Baberton Mains didn't take too long. The Saturday rush hadn't started yet. The afternoon traffic would intensify after lunch when people had sobered up and wondered what to do with themselves only a month and a half before Christmas.

'When's your ex-wife coming back for her car?' Alex said from the passenger seat.

'Who knows? Meantime, I'll keep using it.'

He drove along Queensferry Road, skirting the city centre altogether. 'I wonder what all of this puzzle stuff means?'

'I haven't a clue. I can't even do Sudoku.'

He laughed. 'I bet you can't.'

'I'm serious; all those numbers, trying to get them in order one way, then another. Jesus, it should be listed as an instrument of torture.'

'You're not into figures, then?'

'I am not! Bloody figures. I hated maths at school. I was lucky to get through the police exam. I mean, I passed, but my numerical skills aren't going to set the world on fire.'

After coming off the bypass, he drove along Calder Road then up Wester Hailes Road, entering Baberton from the bottom.

A few minutes later, he turned into Maggie Carlton's street. And was blocked by the fire engines.

'Jesus,' Harry said, when he looked over at the smouldering wreck of what had been Maggie Carlton's house.

They got out and walked over to the commander in charge of the scene. They showed their warrant cards.

'What happened here?'

'Don't you know? I thought your colleagues had called you out.' He indicated at a uniformed patrol parked across the street.

'No, we came here looking for the occupant.'

'Well, you might be out of luck. We found a body. Not burnt, but she probably died from smoke inhalation.'

The roof was burnt off and the walls were a blackened shell. 'Is there ID on the body?' Alex asked.

'She was already outside being attended to by a doctor but it was too late.'

'What sort of fire would do that?' Harry said.

'An accelerated one. Some liquid, not petrol, but maybe lighter fluid, or white spirit. Something got it going well and good though.'

'Has the body been removed yet?'

'Yes. She was taken away a little while ago.'

'What time did the call come in for this?'

'A little after five thirty.'

Harry thanked the man and they walked over to one of the uniforms; he was recognised before he could show his ID.

'Since this fire is suspicious, do you have any witnesses?' Harry doubted anybody would be walking around on a cold, dark Saturday morning in Baberton Mains, unless they were a ne'er-do-well.

'One man across the road...' he turned and pointed out onto the main road, across from the cul-de-sac, 'got up for a pee around five-thirty. His daughter was staying over with a friend, and he noticed headlights through his curtains. Nothing unusual in that, but he thought maybe his daughter had changed her mind, and had decided to come home. She's in her twenties and was in the town on a night out.

'Anyway, he peeked through the curtains and saw a black Range Rover parked with its lights on in the cul-de-sac. The flames were already licking through the roof and the car backed out at high speed.'

'I don't suppose he got a number plate?' Alex asked.

'No, ma'am. And when we got the call to come here, the duty doc was already here and he had pronounced her. Then the mortuary crew turned up and took her away.'

'Which house?' Harry said. The uniform pointed again. Harry and Alex made their way to the house and rang the doorbell. The sun was out but it was teasing them, offering them no warmth as a wind blasted across the road.

A woman answered and looked out at them with a hint of suspicion, as if they were the fireraisers come to do her house next.

'We're police officers. Could we have a word?'

'Oh, yes, come in.' She let them in and closed the door to keep the heat in.

'Would you like a coffee?' she said as she led them into the living room. It was spotless. Nothing was lying around and Harry had seen dirtier show homes.

'No, thank you. Can we take a note of your name?'

'Carol Mathers. You can sit down, if you like.'

They sat down on the pristine couch, Harry looking for any dirt he might have tracked into the woman's house, sure she would be right out with the hoover after they'd left.

'I believe your husband may have seen something in the early hours of this morning, in regard to the fire across the road,' Harry said.

'He said he did. He'd been round at the golf club. It's just through the trees next to the house that was on fire, but you can't walk through that way of course. Anyway, he and his pals have a good drink there on a Friday night, which means he has to get up for a pee through the night. When he was up this morning, he saw headlights, and since he's a nosy bugger, he looked out the window and saw a strange car in the driveway. Then shortly after that, we heard something, like wood crackling. We looked out and saw the house on fire. But the car was gone.'

'Have either of you seen a car like that at the house before?'

'I'm not nosy, son, so I wouldn't know. My husband is and he said he hadn't seen anything like that around here before. But we saw a taxi leave the street. Maybe he saw something.'

'A black cab?' Harry asked.

The woman nodded her response. 'There are a few of them live around here though, but who knows?'

'What about the woman who lives there? Do you know her to talk to?'

'Only in the passing. There used to be the two of

them living there, sisters I think, but I've only seen the one recently.' She took a deep breath and blew it out again. 'I saw them take the body away in that van. God bless her.'

'Have you seen anybody suspicious lurking about recently?' Alex asked.

'Not that I can think of. It's a very quiet place. We don't get much trouble here at all.'

Harry stood up and took a business card out of his wallet and handed it to her. 'If you can think of anything else, please don't hesitate to call.'

Outside, the cold hit them after the warmth of the house. 'That bloody Range Rover gets about,' Harry said.

'It might have been that taxi. Big, black car. My husband was probably still drunk. It was dark. Who knows.'

'If I see that baldy bastard again, I'll be having a wee chat with him.'

'Make sure you have Simon Gregg with you,' Alex said.

'Meaning what?'

'That you're of a smaller stature and not as young.'

'The bigger they are, and all that.'

'That's bollocks, Harry. The bigger they are, the more chance you're going to get a ride in the back of an ambulance.'

'Still. I owe baldy a wee talking to, and if he's not with his motorcycle chums, we'll be having that talk.' His phone rang and he answered it. 'Hello?'

'DCI McNeil? It's Maggie Carlton. We really need to talk.'

ELEVEN

'I should go back to my own flat tonight,' Alex said as Harry drove along Slateford, following the shopping centre brigade.

'Okay.'

'*No, no, Alex, I insist you stay at my place,*' she said.

'I didn't want to sound like I was desperate for you to stay.'

'Like you were some kind of perv trying to take advantage of a younger colleague?'

'Something like that.'

'Or are you worried that Vanessa might see me and wonder what's going on?'

'I couldn't care bloody less what she thinks. She took herself out of my life so she can sod off. Of course you can stay tonight. Stay as long as you want until we get those bastards.'

Harry felt himself getting revved up, now more than anything wanting to have a word with the little bastard who he had knocked off the motorbike.

'I was just joking. About staying. I should just go back.' She looked sideways at him for a moment as he navigated round a bus that was pulling into a stop.

'It's your call. There's nobody else using the spare bedroom, and I don't want to be one of those condescending men who think that women can't look after themselves, but there's a team of them, and if they come at us, I think we'd have a better chance if there was the two of us.'

'You have a good point. You've talked me into it.'

'There was no *talking you into it* bollocks. The decision is yours.'

'Okay, Harry, I'll stay, if you insist.'

'You know, sometimes I pray for God to take me in my sleep. Just so I won't have to listen to your gums flapping.'

'That's the nicest thing a man has ever said to me.'

'You never give up, do you?'

'Nope. It's one of my best qualities.' She grinned at him.

He found a parking space in the underground car park of the flats and they got to the door just in time for Maggie Carlton to answer it.

'I have to say, I was surprised when you called me,'

Harry said as they went through into the living room. 'You know about your house?'

She looked blankly at him. 'What about it?'

'I'm sorry to have to tell you this but your house was set on fire overnight. They found somebody inside. We thought it was you.'

'What?' Maggie stopped for a second. 'Was it deliberate?'

'That's what they're thinking.'

'Where's Bea?' Alex said.

'I'm not sure. I just woke a little while ago. Last night, I was in Fiona's room. Bea made me a cuppa and the next thing I know, I'm waking up on top of Fiona's bed.'

'Go and check on her,' Harry said to Alex.

She walked through to the hallway and knocked on Bea's bedroom door, opening it when there was no answer.

Harry stood looking at the photographs on the shelf again. There were none of Bea, but there were one or two of Fiona Carlton with a young man. Harry took photos of them with his phone.

'She's not in,' Alex said when she came right back. 'Maybe she went to work?'

'Maybe. We didn't have much of a conversation.'

'How long have you known her?' Harry asked Maggie.

'Just a couple of months. Although I wouldn't say I *knew* her. Just to say hi to. I wasn't round here a lot.'

'Did she have a car?'

'No, she said she didn't want to drive in the city.'

'Then how did she get out to the Bush Estate to work?'

'The bus. She didn't have to go out there often. The company promotes *artistic independence*. McCallum didn't want his staff to feel stifled by working in their offices. We have to go in every couple of weeks for a conference to discuss what they were working on, but as long as we do the work at home and sent it in every night, he was happy.'

'Did you ever hear anything about her at work?'

'No. I work in a different department. Although we technically do the same job, we're working on different projects. And we're not allowed to talk to people in other projects.'

'Did Bea have a boyfriend?'

'I wouldn't know. But I did see her out with an older man in the pub one night.'

'Can you describe him?' Harry said.

'Fifties, maybe. Bald. Heavily built.'

'Do you have anywhere you can stay?' Harry asked. 'If your clothes were upstairs in your house, then it's all gone.'

'I could call HR and see if they'll let me stay here. I'm sure it will be fine. I'll have to go shopping.'

'Bea won't mind you staying?' Alex asked.

'She doesn't have a choice.'

'Does anybody else know you're here?' Harry asked.

'Not that I'm aware.'

'Just be aware of your surroundings, and don't go near your house. The fire investigators are all over it.'

His phone rang. He spoke to the caller before hanging up.

'We have to go. If you need me at short notice, please don't hesitate to call me.' He handed her a card.

'Thank you.'

Back down in the car park, Harry started up the Honda. 'That was Kate Murphy at the mortuary. There's something she wanted to show us.'

TWELVE

The mortuary had a distinct quiet air about it as Harry and Alex entered through the back door.

They were met by Angie Patterson, who smiled when she saw Harry. 'Dr Murphy is waiting for you upstairs in the PM suite.'

'Thanks, Angie.'

'When I'm not on-call, maybe we could all go out for a Chinese and something to drink?' she said, smiling.

'Of course. You up for that?' he said to Alex.

'I suppose.'

'Her enthusiasm knows no bounds. But yes, I'm up for it.'

They went upstairs in the lift and Kate Murphy was waiting for them. 'Hello, Harry.'

'Morning, doc,' he replied, looking at his watch and

seeing it was well after lunchtime. 'Well, it was morning when I got up.'

'There's something very odd going on,' Kate said, cutting to the chase.

'What's wrong?'

'You'd better come into our small conference room. I have something to show you.'

Inside, the room was functional, with a rectangular table and chairs round it, and a TV sitting on a cabinet at one end.

'God knows how we're going to explain this one away, but here we go. Take a seat. You're going to need it.'

They all sat, Kate near the front with the remote control which she pointed it at the screen and it came to life. 'Before I start the show, let me fill you in. Angie was on call, and she got the call to go to a house fire in Baberton early this morning. When she got there, the force doctor on duty was there and he said he had pronounced the death. The woman was life extinct. The strange thing was, he had already put her in the body bag. He helped lift her into the van. Then Angie brought her here, and put her right into the fridge. The other assistants would take her out first thing Monday morning and have her prepared for post-mortem. Until this happened. Angie went out on another call. Just watch.'

Cameras were inside the loading area and all around the lower level of the mortuary. They saw the Judas door open and two men walk in. Kate pressed *pause* and the image froze.

'The one on the right is the force doctor who pronounced our victim at the scene. He was there when Angie turned up. Do either of you recognise him?'

'No. It's old Doc Wilson who's one of the duty doctors. That man isn't one of ours, that I know of,' Harry said.

'I haven't seen him either,' Alex said.

'He wasn't worried about hiding his identity,' Kate said. 'The CCTV cameras had been put out of action before the man came to the mortuary. All the council ones. They're all on a circuit. They were knocked out. However, last year, at Halloween, somebody broke in to steal a body, but they abandoned the idea after gaining entry. The council put up an independent CCTV system that doesn't run on Wi-Fi or Bluetooth or whatever. We have cameras all over the place now. The feed goes right into a recorder. I'm assuming they thought they'd knocked out all the cameras, but they hadn't obviously.'

She started playing the tape again. The men walked through to the refrigeration area and switched the lights on. Then one of them pulled open the drawer that the fire victim was put in. He unzipped the bag and opened it up. They all clearly saw the face of the victim; had a look inside before zipping it back up again.

Then the men took an end each and carried it outside and put it into the back of a black van.

'We know the victim,' Harry said. 'Her name is Bea Anderson.'

'That's strange; that's not what her ID says.'

'What ID?'

'Her warrant card. And this is where it gets weird and why I called you personally. The first officer on the scene got a look at the warrant card before putting it back in her pocket. He thought you knew about it when you turned up at the fire. But when Angie logged her in, there was no ID on her.'

'What? What did the warrant card say?'

Kate looked at Alex. 'DS Alexis Maxwell.'

THIRTEEN

'And you've no idea why she would have your ID on her?' Harry said, pulling the car into the spot outside the front door of McCallum Technology.

'For the ninety-ninth time, I do not know why she had a warrant card in my name. I still have mine on me.'

'What happens when I ask for the hundredth time?'

'Go ahead and pull the trigger on that one, find out for yourself.'

'I'll wait 'til there's some distance between us. Maybe I'll call and ask you.'

'Considering I'm going to be staying at your place again tonight, that would be very wise.'

He locked the car and shrugged into his overcoat as the wind whipped across the open parkland. 'Seriously though, somebody seems to know a lot about you. They know where you live. They know your name and rank.'

'I thought there was something dodgy about her. Then when Maggie Carlton told us this morning that she had fallen asleep and was out for the count until this morning, then it crossed my mind that Bea had slipped Maggie something.'

'So Maggie wouldn't see or hear anything.' Harry shook his head. He'd known men who had done that on a night out with the roofies, but this was different.

Inside, they went through the rigmarole of getting into the building to speak with somebody. And once again James McCallum appeared in his wheelchair, as if by magic, Max Blue by his side.

'You must like this place,' McCallum said with a smile.

'I've been to worse places,' Harry said.

'My front-end staff tell me you're looking for information on a certain member of staff. Unfortunately, HR don't work at the weekend.'

'You don't seem to mind putting the hours in,' Alex said to him.

'I live on the premises. In a house just along from here. With my staff. Max lives here too, but in his own place.'

'And who do we have here?' a blonde woman said, approaching them.

'Chief Inspector McNeil, may I introduce my wife, Melissa McCallum.'

Harry shook hands with her and introduced Alex.

'What can we help you with today?' Melissa asked. 'Are we in trouble?'

'Have you done something wrong?'

Melissa grinned. 'I don't believe we have.'

'Then I won't be slapping the cuffs on today. But we need some information about an employee of yours.'

'What's the name?'

'Bea Anderson.'

'The name doesn't ring a bell, but I can certainly find out what you need. We have plenty of staff working today. Not HR, but I'm sure we can find somebody. Max? Why don't you help me while my husband entertains Police Scotland's finest?'

'Jolly good idea!' McCallum said. 'I was going over to the track. You can come and watch.' He manoeuvred his wheelchair round a series of corners, Harry and Alex following him while Melissa and Max made their way upstairs.

'Have you done any more research on self-driving cars, Harry?' McCallum said. 'You don't mind me calling you Harry, do you?'

'That's fine. And no, I haven't done any research.'

'It's a fascinating subject. May I ask, do either of you have children?'

'I have a son.'

'I don't have any yet,' Alex said, and Harry thought he could detect a hint of regret in her voice. He wondered if she was thinking about her fiancé and what could have been if he had kept it in his pants instead of messing about on her. Maybe she would have had children by now.

They reached a back door and went through a security area with guards. Then they could see the disabled van waiting for McCallum. He drove his wheelchair in through the side door and motioned for them to follow him.

There were smaller seats that they sat on and the driver climbed in behind the wheel.

'Harry, how old is your son?' McCallum asked.

'Just turned sixteen.'

'And keen to get behind the wheel of a car, no doubt?'

'He can't wait.'

The van took off slowly, left the private car park round the back of the house and the driver drove along a one-way road with hedges bordering it. There were new buildings peeking up above the hedges.

'I was like that. All gung-ho, can't wait to go speeding around with my friends, showing off. And I did. But that's not how I ended up in a wheelchair. Oh no, that one wasn't my fault at all.'

They drove into an open area with a lot more vehicles around. The mention of McCallum in his wheelchair had killed the conversation for a moment.

'You would want your son to be as safe as possible, Harry, yes?' McCallum said as the van stopped.

'Of course.'

'Then one day he will be. Along with the rest of humanity. Oh, don't get me wrong, it's not going to happen tomorrow, but it is coming. Look at the technology from ten years ago. It was utter garbage. Yes, we put men on the moon fifty years ago, but even a luxury car has more computing power than those rockets. It's just a matter of harnessing the new technology in the right way, and we here at McCallum Technology have harnessed that power. And it is not a case of Icarus flying into the sun, I can assure you. But come, let me show you rather than tell you.'

The driver had lowered the ramp and McCallum drove himself down, expertly guiding the wheelchair.

They looked at a small hangar as McCallum drove himself across to it, the driver not very far away. Harry suspected the man was more than just a driver, and probably an expert in taking out somebody's eyeball with a thumb should anybody get close to the boss.

There were several people carriers sitting outside the hangar. 'What do you see there, Harry?'

'Some cars.'

'Exactly. Some ordinary looking cars, would you say?'

'I would.'

He pulled up the collar on his coat. 'Come on, let's step into the office.'

The office was a modern building with a ramp at the front. Inside, it was warm and clean, just how Harry expected it would be. McCallum turned to them. 'You see those new offices we just passed? That's where the real brains of the operation are. We have a new building behind Bush House, where a lot of our computer engineering goes on, but then their work is sent into those offices, and more nerds work on the ideas. Then it goes to the underground lab that I told you about yesterday. Then that work is forwarded to here. The next step? Out on the road. But watch.'

He led them through to a suite where banks of monitors were attached to a wall.

'Larry! Let's get this show on the road,' McCallum shouted to a man in a lab coat.

'Yes, sir.'

McCallum nudged Harry in the leg. 'Keep your eye on the eighty-five-inch screen in the middle.'

The image showed a view out of one of the people carriers.

'Have you seen those American cars on YouTube, Harry?' McCallum asked. 'The self-driving ones, I mean.'

'Can't say I have.'

'They have these stupid things sitting on the roof of their cars. The brains of the operation. What we've done here is scaled things down a bit. No added modifications like that, no big boxes on the roof. No, we've gone a step ahead of that.'

'Several steps ahead,' Larry the lab man said, looking at the boss like he thought McCallum was going to argue with him.

'Several steps. I stand corrected. You wouldn't think I was the one who was responsible for giving them a job. See how they treat me? Contradict me at every turn, show me little respect.'

'No respect,' Larry interrupted.

'See? If Larry wasn't so good at his job, I'd...'

Harry stared at McCallum, waiting to see what was going to come out of his mouth next.

'...fire his arse out the door.' He pointed to the screen. 'Now watch.'

There was a camera inside the car, facing out, as though a GoPro was attached to the driver's head.

'This is an earlier demonstration we did a few months ago. To compare with what we have now.'

The people carrier was driving on a road, going through the trees.

'That's a private test track. It's not a public road, so don't worry.' McCallum sat back in his chair, a smile on his face as he anticipated what was going to happen next.

The car was getting up to speed, a canopy of trees overhead, putting the road into shadow. The speed increased to fifty mph. The road disappeared into a right-hand turn and the car was slowing down, when a big four by four came around on the people carrier's side of the road. At high speed.

Suddenly, it was right in front of the vehicle and hit it head on. There was an explosion of glass, the airbags erupted and there was a sensation of the back of the car being lifted up into the air while pieces of the interior flew about unhindered.

'The big SUV was going at seventy miles an hour. The driver didn't have his seatbelt on and he died at the scene. The driver of the people carrier was doing less than the speed limit, but despite the driver having his belt on, he was severely injured.'

Harry looked at the man and saw a tear running out of one eye and realised he had been describing his own crash.

'The driver of the people carrier was left handi-capped for the rest of his life while his young son and wife were both killed.'

'This is a recreation of that crash?' Alex said.

'It is. When we created the tracks, both the open ones and the forest ones, I wanted the part of that road recreated down to the last detail, and the engineers made it happen. My own accident happened down in England. The man who died had fought with his girl-friend and had been drinking. He was five times over the limit. Later on, his girlfriend said that her boyfriend had left, saying he was going to kill somebody. That somebody was himself and my family.'

'I'm sorry to hear that,' Alex said.

McCallum wiped the tear away and smiled at her. 'Don't be. A lot of good has come out of it. I put my heart and soul into working on this new technology and now I have a lot of good, clever people working for me. Except Larry. He's a cheeky bugger.'

Larry turned and gave McCallum a thumbs up.

'But let me show you the difference now.' He nodded to Larry, who tapped a man on the shoulder, somebody who was sitting down at the consoles. There were other people next to him and it was like being privy to a space launch. He hoped it wouldn't be a case of, *Houston, we have a problem.*

This view was now out the windscreen of one of

the people carriers that had been sitting outside the hangar. It moved slowly along the track and then it got up to speed just as it entered the forest section. It was obeying the speed limit and keeping on its own side of the road. After a few minutes, it was entering the same spot where the accident had happened. Then they saw the lights of an oncoming people carrier and Harry thought they were going to crash again, but the vehicle sailed on by without any hint of a problem.

'Both of those cars are driving themselves. There is nobody behind the wheel. There are people in them, checking diagnostics and the like, but the cars are thinking for themselves. If that had been a self-driving vehicle that had come round the corner that night, my wife and son would still be here.'

'It's impressive,' Harry said without much conviction.

'I'm sure you've seen the news stories where those self-driving cars have crashed, and people have died?'

'I have indeed.'

'People wonder why self-driving cars are involved in crashes. The answer is simple; people don't obey the rules of the road, but the self-driving cars do. For example, you might have a self-driving car stop at a stop sign, but the person behind wasn't intending to, and he's expecting the car in front to slide on through, but it doesn't, and the car in front ends up getting back-ended.

'That won't happen with our technology. You see, not only are we building the technology to be fitted into every new car, but we're building units that will be retro-fitted to any car that has a computer in it. I'll be lobbying the government to have all cars fitted as matter of law. Nobody else has to die on the roads. Of course, they will, until our technology hits every car.'

'That's powerful stuff,' Alex said. 'Can you imagine all the accidents that wouldn't happen every year?'

'Yes, I can. No accidents on the roads means that we're also freeing up time for the ambulance services, and the hospitals. The government will be saving a fortune on the NHS if they adopt our technology.'

'You just have to convince them to use it, right?' Harry said.

'Yes, we do. We've had representatives come here and see it for themselves, and so far, they've been impressed.'

'Not everybody's going to be convinced,' Alex said.

'People are sceptical about everything. Think back fifty years. Well, I know we can't because I'm sure you're not even thirty, but once upon a time, VHS was thrust upon us, then the CD and then digital music. Computers used to cost a fortune, but now every child has one in his or her hand every day. The mobile phone. And laptops, and iPads. The list goes on. Artificial intelligence is coming for us, and those of us who aren't at the front trying to harness it, will be left on the floor. By the time young kids today grow up, they will be used to the new technology, so self-driving cars won't be so far-fetched for them.'

'What other kind of AI do you research?' Alex asked.

'Sorry, I can't talk about that. It's for the government, so it's classified.'

'Fair enough.'

On the screen, two people carriers were driving at high speed towards each other, but before they even got close, both vehicles slowed down and stopped.

'That's a scenario where there is traffic following the other car and they are both talking to each other. The one on the wrong side of the road is an older vehicle which has been retrofitted with the new computers. It was still able to talk to the new vehicle and both vehicles knew what was going on in a matter of seconds and did something to prevent a crash.'

McCallum was smiling again, then the smile slipped a little bit as his mind transported him back to the night his family were killed.

'How long before we actually see these vehicles on the roads?' Harry asked.

'Five years. Legislation moves at a snail's pace, but we're heading in the right direction, and the technology is getting tweaked every day. In another five years, these cars you see today will be the VHS of cars, and the CDs will be taking over.'

'What about digital?' Alex said, smiling.

'The world won't be ready for digital in five years. Maybe ten, but by then, we'll be so far advanced.'

They all turned to look at McCallum's wife walking towards them. 'He's been showing you his toys, I take it?' Melissa said, smiling at them.

'He has indeed,' Harry said.

'Anyway, I asked somebody to do some checking, and it turns out that nobody called Bea Anderson works here.'

'She said she worked from home, but was employed by the company.'

'Sorry. Nobody by that name has *ever* worked here.'

FOURTEEN

The four-piece band were the typical private club quartet, doing numbers that would appeal to everybody, except maybe for the younger generation who were into acid house, or whatever it was called.

'Same again?' he said to Alex.

'I'll get them, Harry. We don't want the regulars to think you've brought some floozy here to show her off.'

'That ship already sailed. I saw one of the committee members giving you the eye earlier.'

'He was astounded to see you with such a beautiful woman.' She smiled at him.

'He's got cataracts, but whatever keeps you off the bridge.'

She nudged him and went up to the bar.

'Harry! How lovely to see you!' a female voice said

from behind him. 'Bowling season might be over, but socialising on a Saturday night certainly isn't.'

He turned to see one of the bowling club's committee members, a woman in her late fifties, who was still struggling to come to terms with turning forty, if her short dress was anything to go by.

'Rena. I haven't seen you for ages.'

'Not so much since you and Vanessa split. In fact, we've seen more of her now that she has a new... friend.'

'Boyfriend, Rena. I know all about him.'

Rena laughed and sat down beside him. 'Is that what she told you?'

'I saw him for myself, just last night.'

'Well, unless they've accelerated their relationship, I was led to believe that he's just a friend of hers. And I should know, being the gossipy old cow that I am.'

Harry couldn't help but laugh. 'Hardly old, Rena.'

She guffawed and gently slapped his arm. 'Trust me, if she's pretending to have a boyfriend, then she's playing games with you. But sticking with the nosy cow theme, I haven't seen that young lady with you before.'

'She's my colleague, nothing more. DS Alex Maxwell.'

'She seems nice.'

'She is, but I don't want you talking to her and spoiling the illusion about me.'

'She's not your next conquest then?' Rena said with a grin.

'We're just friends.'

'Friends with benefits. You can tell old Rena, Harry. Go on, make my day, spill the juicy gossip.'

'Well, I heard that Waitrose round the corner is going to put the price of beans up, but I can't confirm.'

'Oh, you're such a wicked boy. Wait 'til I see your mother next.'

'Seriously, Alex and I are just colleagues.'

'That's why you're in the bowling club with her on a Saturday night? You've got a long way to go before you can pull the wool over Rena's eyes. But enjoy yourself. Life's too short. Look at me. My Stu's been gone two years now and do you think I've had a bite?'

'The dating game can be dangerous, Rena.'

'Not if you go out with a copper.'

'If I didn't know you better, I'd think you were hitting on me.'

'Oh, you damn well know I'm hitting on you, Harry McNeil. If I was twenty years younger, we could get tangled up in your duvet, but at my age, I'd settle for wrinkling the sheets a bit.' She laughed again. 'But here's some advice from an old bint who's been round the block a few times; don't let any woman get under your skin. Especially Vanessa. And by God, if I hear her badmouthing you in here, then her arse will be barred before the door bangs it on her way out.'

He squeezed her hand. 'I'm glad I have you in my corner.'

'Hello,' Alex said, coming back with the drinks.

Harry made the introductions.

Rena stood up. 'Don't worry, honey, we weren't about to start snogging. Me and Harry go way back.'

Alex smiled. 'Don't let me stop you. Harry and I just work with each other.'

'Keep an eye on him, doll. His last one was into playing mind games, and that's not something I find acceptable.' Rena stood taller than Alex and when she wasn't smiling, she presented a formidable force.

'I'll certainly look out for him.'

'Just remember, Vanessa has some friends in here too, people who will smile at your face and stab you in the back, Harry. I'll bet one of them has already been on the phone to her about you being in here.'

'Thanks, Rena. I'll bear that in mind.'

'Good. Now where's old Bill? He promised me a dance and I think he's avoiding me.' She looked around. 'No, there he is. Another few Bells and I'm sure he'll be up for buying me a fish supper. Catch you later, Harry. Good meeting you, Alex.'

'Likewise.'

They watched Rena make her way over to an older man who was smiling as Rena approached.

'I hope he doesn't care if his duvet gets shredded tonight,' Harry said.

Alex looked puzzled.

'Never mind. What was it you were saying before you went to the bar?' He raised his glass in salute and they clinked glasses.

'I think somehow, Bea Anderson was connected to the break-in at my house. I mean, she was there when I said I was taking the computer home, she had a warrant card on her with my name on it, and now she's turned up dead.'

'She lived with Fiona Carlton, who had a flash drive in her shoe with information on it that could have been connected to the schematics on the computer they wanted. It's like they were living in the same flat and Bea wanted what Fiona had, but she didn't know exactly where it was or how to get it.'

'I want a background check done first thing on Monday morning. Give the new lassie something to do. What's her name again?'

'Eve Bell,' Harry said.

'Aye. Eve Bell. Let's see what she's made of.'

'I'd like Simon Gregg to check out the CCTV near the canal basin.'

Alex was talking to him but looking at the front door of the club. 'Isn't that what's-her-name?'

'Who?'

'Her nibs.'

'Again, who are you talking about?' He didn't turn his head in the direction that Alex was looking, but his heart started beating a little faster. He knew damn well who she was talking about. He lifted the pint glass to his lips and turned his head slowly. Shite. Vanessa, Queen of the Darkness, was walking in with a friend of hers. Not her boyfriend, or fake boyfriend whoever the hell he was, but some busty blonde with a laugh that would strip wallpaper.

'Christ. Drink up, we're leaving,' he said, starting to chug at his pint.

'Will you calm down? She's already playing head games with you, so why don't you play her at her own game?'

'How do I do that? Dance with you on a table?'

'No, but you could sit here and smile and show her that it's none of her business, you being here with a colleague. Fuck her, Harry, I'm not being intimidated.'

'You know what? I'm doing nothing wrong. Let her look.'

Suddenly, Rena was at his shoulder again. 'Just give the signal, Harry, and I will rip her a new arsehole.

People like you in here, but nobody would be lining up to urinate on Vanessa if she spontaneously combusted.' She smiled at Alex. 'You look after him, honey. Don't let Miss *Butter wouldn't melt in my mouth* there play with him.'

'Way ahead of you there, Rena.'

Rena smiled and patted Harry on the shoulder. 'She's a keeper, Harry.'

'She's just...' he started to say, but Rena was walking away.

'Just what?' Alex said, smiling.

'You're enjoying this, aren't you?'

'Immensely.'

Harry watched as Vanessa and her friend got a drink and squeezed in at a table on the other side of the room. *Fuck it* he thought and held out his hand to Alex.

'You want to dance?'

'I thought you'd never ask.'

FIFTEEN

'Never again,' Harry said, standing at the kitchen sink, washing down a couple of pills he'd found in the cupboard, hoping they were aspirin and not some left-over birth control pills. He'd put his dressing gown on and was leaning on the kitchen counter when Alex appeared.

'Good morning.' She was smiling at him as she put the kettle on.

'What in the name of God happened last night?'

'First of all, you were adding a chaser to every pint you had, even though I mildly suggested you might want to slow down, but your reply went along the lines of, *Vanessa can go fuck herself.* Then you put your arm around my shoulders to steady yourself just before you puked your load onto a neighbour's hedge.'

'No. Tell me you're yanking my chain.'

She laughed again. 'There is no chain yanking going on, I can assure you. But let me finish; you came upstairs and wanted to crack a bottle of wine, but I talked you out of it. My dad always warned about mixing the grapes with the hops. Or something like that, but you get the idea. No wine, then you started falling about the place and yes, I did take your trousers off to get you into bed.'

He started to say something but she held up a hand. 'I'm not finished. By *getting you into bed* I meant that in the literal sense, and don't worry, I've seen a grown man in his skids before.'

'Christ. Is my face red? It feels like it's on fire.'

'I then put your covers on you, and just so there is no ambiguity, no, we did not do anything we shouldn't have done last night. Your reputation remains intact. Mine, however, might be in tatters. Vanessa was standing looking at you as we crossed the road.'

'How come my skids were on backwards when I woke up, then?' He finished the glass of water.

'Harry, what you do in the privacy of your own room is your business.'

'Seriously, thanks for seeing me home. God knows what I was thinking.'

'You were trying to metaphorically poke Vanessa in the eye.'

'I need a shower.'

'I'll do you a coffee when you get out. I know how you like it. You want some breakfast?'

He waved as he left the kitchen. When he came back, showered and dressed, she made his coffee and made herself another one.

'I hope my snoring didn't interrupt your sleep,' he said.

'It didn't. The man outside with the chainsaw running all night woke me up once or twice.'

'I've been known to snore on the odd occasion.'

She laughed. 'I'm just kidding. Those G&Ts put me out like a light. Of course, I drank within my limitations and I feel fine this morning.'

Harry's mobile phone rang and he thought it might be *that woman from across the road* as Alex described Vanessa now. It wasn't. He listened to the caller before hanging up.

'As if my head isn't hurting enough.'

'What's wrong?'

'That was control. We're needed down at the mortuary. Somebody broke in again.'

Alex pulled in behind the patrol cars and the forensics van. There were other cars in the small car park.

'This is probably the busiest Sunday they've seen

117

in a long time,' Harry said as they made their way inside.

'You weren't here a couple of Christmases ago,' Kate Murphy said, leading them through to the refrigeration room. 'We were full to overflowing. We had to wrap them up and stack them on the floor.'

'Typhoid Mary in town that year?' Harry said.

'It was bitterly cold and a lot of homeless people died.'

'Gotcha.' He excused himself for a moment and found the drinking fountain outside the bathroom door. The door opened and DC Simon Gregg came out. Harry jumped. 'Christ, I thought it was one of them come back from the dead.'

'Sorry, boss,' Gregg said, grinning. 'Were you out on the lash last night? Your eyes are all red.'

'No, I was just crying at the thought of seeing you on a Sunday.'

'They say a hair of the dog is good for when you've *been crying*.' He ended the sentence with air quotes.

'Just show me what's been happening here, Gregg.'

'This way.' He led Harry back to the fridges where Kate Murphy was standing with Angie Patterson.

'Kate was just saying how they had to be professionals,' Alex said. 'The people who broke in here. They left no marks on the door. The CCTV system was disabled again.'

'And no doubt they were driving a big, black car.' He turned to Gregg. 'See what businesses near here have outside CCTV. Take what help you need. The hotel at the foot of St Mary's Street will probably have some.'

'What timeframe are we looking at?' Gregg asked.

Harry looked at Kate.

'Well, Angie was on-call and there were two deaths through the night. One person was stabbed and there was a man who is a sudden death. Heart attack, more than likely. Then nothing else. He was logged in here at six thirty am. That's when Angie noticed the Judas door was open. She didn't want to come in on her own and did the right thing by calling treble nine.' She looked at Angie. 'That sounds about right, doesn't it?'

'Yes, that's right. The stabbing victim was brought here because he pronounced dead at the scene, and he was logged in at one thirty this morning.'

Harry turned to Gregg. 'There you have your five-hour window. Get at it.'

'Sir.'

Harry watched as Gregg walked away, taking one of the uniforms with him.

'That's not all,' Kate said. 'The worst is still to come.'

Harry looked puzzled.

'Both of you come upstairs to the conference room. I'll show you there.'

She started playing the footage. 'The council's CCTV cameras had been fixed, but they cut them off again. Thank goodness we have the extra coverage from the secure system.'

They watched as two men came in. One was bigger built than the other.

'Looks like a different man this time.'

'Looks like it,' Kate said, 'but watch what they do next.'

All eyes were on the large screen as the two people put on scrubs, then they opened another drawer and pulled out a corpse. The sheet was pulled down to reveal Fiona Carlton's lifeless body. They loaded her onto a trolley and wheeled her to the lift, taking her up to the post-mortem suite.

Kate played around with the buttons on the remote and then they saw the view from inside the post mortem room itself with the stainless steel tables sitting in a row. Fiona Carlton was wheeled in and her body moved onto one of the tables. The sheet was removed entirely. Then one of them wheeled over a stainless steel stand that had surgical tools on it. He lifted a scalpel while the bigger man watched, then he expertly cut into the corpse. The man reached his hands into the stomach and rummaged around, like a medical student who hadn't been paying attention.

'Jesus,' Alex said.

After a few minutes, he was finished and walked over to a sink to wash his gloved hands before taking them off. Then they walked out and the cameras followed them downstairs. They took off their scrubs, left them on the floor and walked out.

The outside view showed them getting into a black Range Rover.

'Good God,' Harry said.

'I know. It's horrific,' Kate said. 'They just left Fiona where she was, on the table.'

'That man. We've seen him before, driving that big car.' He looked at Alex. 'And from the pub.'

'You're right, that *is* him. One of the men who attacked us Friday night at my house.'

'They steal a corpse first, then come back for a DIY post-mortem. What the hell are they doing?' Kate asked.

'And where have they hidden the corpse they stole?'

SIXTEEN

'Your head feeling any better?' Alex asked as she drove them up to Fountainbridge.

'It's starting to feel like it's attached to my neck now.'

'I hadn't realised what a drinking machine you were,' she said, pulling into the underground car park at Lower Gilmore Place. 'And you're sure you actually spoke to Maggie Carlton on the phone and hadn't dialled Santa's hotline by mistake?'

He looked at her. 'I have used a mobile phone before, you know.'

'Well, at least we know what list you'll be on when you finally do get around to calling Santa.'

Upstairs, Maggie Carlton opened the door. She looked like she hadn't slept much, and Harry wondered if the young woman now kept a cricket bat beside her bed.

'Have you found Fiona's killer?' she asked.

'No, we haven't. We were hoping you might have some more information on Bea.'

They sat down, Harry glad to get the weight off his feet. Normally, he'd still be in bed, ready to go out for a quick pint with Vanessa at lunchtime. He mentally kicked himself for even thinking her name.

'I'm not sure I have anything to add.' She was sitting on a chair with her legs pulled up and put her arms round her knees.

'How long had Bea lived here?' Alex asked.

'I already told you, I'm not sure. Fiona lived with me in my house. A couple of months ago, she came to live here.'

Harry nodded. '*Why* did Fiona move here?'

Maggie looked at the floor. Said nothing.

'Was that her stuff you were burning in your back garden?'

Maggie looked at him. 'Not exactly. It was just some rubbish she'd left behind. But we'd had an argument before she left.'

'That must have been hard for you, Fiona being your sister,' Alex said.

'It was. We were arguing over her friend, who she insisted was just a friend, but I didn't believe her. I wanted her to stay with me. I thought it would be safer. But she insisted on moving out. She was here first, then Bea moved in. Which could happen at any time. These flats are like dorm rooms; you can have somebody come stay with you at any time. Of the same sex, of course. That's when Bea showed up.'

'What about her boyfriend?' Harry said. 'Didn't Fiona want to move in with him?'

'She told me she didn't have a boyfriend, that he was just a guy from work.'

'Did you know this guy?'

Maggie nodded. 'Dave Pierce. He's nice. He works as a technician at McCallum and he was just another guy at the office, until Fiona started spending more time with him.'

'You didn't know Bea all that well, but you did meet her,' Alex said. 'What was she like to talk to? Did she give you any background about herself?'

'No. It was just general chit-chat. She was new to McCallum Technology. She just started hanging out with Fiona a few months ago, and she worked in a different department from mine.'

'Was there anybody there who Bea was particularly friendly with?' Harry asked.

'I don't really know. I never actually saw her in the building, but I didn't like her much. You know how you take an instant dislike to somebody?'

'Yes,' Alex said. Harry knew she meant Vanessa.

'It was like that. She was sort of cold towards me. I didn't care. It's not as if we were going to hang out in the pub together.'

'Has this friend of Fiona's got an address we can have?'

'I don't know where he lives. I don't know much about him at all.'

'Did he ever come round here when you were here?'

'Once, I think. Months ago.'

'Was Bea here at the time?'

'Not that I remember.'

Harry looked at the woman. He had sat across from police officers he had been investigating, and he could tell when they were lying. He'd seen it so many times in their faces that he knew exactly how to read their body language and the expressions on their faces.

Just like he knew Maggie Carlton was lying to them right now. About what, he didn't know.

But he would find out.

In the car park, Harry put a finger to his lips briefly.

Alex was still on driving duty. Not that he trusted her driving more than his own, but he didn't want an awkward conversation with a traffic cop by telling him to bog off, and refusing to give his license or take a breathalyser. He wasn't one for drinking and driving, and he wasn't about to start now, so he let Alex drive him home.

'Maggie Carlton is up to something,' he said. 'She knows something, but she isn't sharing it with us.'

'We'll have to go and talk to Dave Pierce tomorrow. I'll call McCallum Technology and see about getting his address.'

They got back to Harry's flat and when he got inside, he had a strange feeling. Something wasn't quite right.

And then he realised he was right when he walked into the living room.

Alex's MacBook Pro was sitting on his dining table.

SEVENTEEN

Monday morning, Harry made sure he was up before Alex. He hadn't been able to sleep much, wondering how they could get into his flat. Then again, he'd known sneaky little bastards who could circumvent the most capable of security systems, never mind a front door lock.

Nevertheless, he'd jammed a chair under the front door handle.

'I thought I'd do some research on my iPad last night,' he said to Alex as she poured some cereal.

'Really? And what were you researching? What wood makes the best chair for shoving under a door handle?'

'You might mock, but it kept us safe, didn't it?'

'I concede your point. But seriously, they have some damn gall coming in here with my old computer.

They're just trying to show us that they know where you live and they can get in anytime.'

'What we need to know is, *why*? Yes, we know there's something on the flash drive they want but why break in here to return the computer? Why not just dump it?'

'As I said, it's a message. They're showing their superiority and no doubt, trying to scare us into the bargain. Maybe I should go round to my place and see if they've been in there again.'

'If we do go there, we go in force. I'll have a couple of patrols with us.'

She sat down at the table opposite him. 'What were you researching?'

'Now that you've got it out of your system, I'll tell you. Artificial intelligence is scary. I have to ask myself, why would we want to build things that will be more intelligent than us? To build machines that will have the power to think independently of us, and then one day take over? The people who do this stuff need to be stopped. It's all ego, like with James McCallum. Clearly, he wants to build a self-driving car that won't allow accidents to happen.'

'Did you Google him?'

'I did, and what I read scares me.'

'Okay. Is he part of some mafia group?'

'You could say that; the AI mafia. The power they

are going to wield is tremendous. The Americans want to get self-driving cars on the road so badly. When you think about it, all the new technology in new cars is all leading up to this. Like lane-keep assist, cars that will brake for you, read speed signs, spot pedestrians. I personally don't think they will perfect it any time soon, but they're close. And what McCallum is doing is going one step further.'

'What do you mean?'

'Right now, the problem is mixing old cars with the new self-driving ones. Everything will be fine when we take driving out of the hands of the humans. And McCallum saw this, that's why he's making units that can be retro-fitted to older cars. Once he corners that market, he'll be laughing all the way to the bank.'

'I think you're right. It's all a pissing contest with these rich people. But I agree, we're still a long way off before we have self-driving cars and proper electric cars. The battery technology just isn't up to speed yet. If it was, we'd all be driving about in electric cars, go into a station to charge up and it would take no longer than it does to fill a petrol tank just now. And then get a thousand-mile range.'

'I think they have the technology already, but the big oil companies have been suppressing it for years. They buy up the patents and file them away, just to line their own pockets. And let's face it, when fossil fuel runs out, it won't matter because they'll slowly be phasing in the new technology and it will be in place when the oil runs dry.'

'I think the car manufacturers are in cahoots with the oil companies. Everybody's scared to take them on. Except for people like James McCallum but even he knows he can't take them on entirely.' Alex felt herself getting fired up. 'The whole oil game was just to screw the public. It had been going on for a very long time, but nobody stood up to them.'

'It still doesn't explain why Bea Anderson was taken out of the mortuary.'

'They're cleaning up behind them?' Alex said.

'I agree.'

Now it was gone ten and the whole team was gathered in the office.

Harry was on his third cup of coffee, despite knowing he'd be visiting the big boys' room more frequently later on.

'Just a recap,' he said, sitting on the corner of a desk. He'd taken his jacket off as the old building was pumping out a fair bit of heat. 'Fiona Carlton was taken out of the Union Canal. She'd been hit over the head with something and stabbed repeatedly. Her sister, Maggie Carlton, had her house set on fire. The woman who Fiona shared a flat with, was found dead in Maggie's house. Somebody went to the mortuary and stole her corpse. The following day, they broke in again and did a rough post-mortem on Fiona. They opened her up. And I have no doubt they were looking for the flash drive that was in her shoe. Maybe they thought she'd swallowed it before she died. Now, what have we got? Eve?'

'We went out yesterday and got some CCTV footage from around the time the woman on the house-boat heard screams. Two hours before and after. And we got lucky with the hotel on Fountainbridge. I'll show you.'

She was sitting at her desk in front of the monitor and they crowded round.

They watched as a man ran down the lane from the canal and crossed over the road and into the hotel. Fiona Carlton was right behind him and she too went into the hotel. Fifteen minutes later, she came back out.

'We lose her going up the lane again,' Eve said. 'Looking at the timeframe, this wouldn't be long before she was murdered.'

'What about the man? Did you get any images from him in the hotel?'

'Yes. More than that though, we got him coming back out. He had booked a room for one night but didn't stay in it. As soon as Fiona left, he checked out. But you'll see him coming out in a minute.'

Harry looked at the face and thought he recognised it. He went through the photos on his phone and looked at the photos he'd taken of the framed photographs in Fiona Carlton's living room.

The CCTV had got a clear photo of his face. 'Print it off. His name's Dave Pierce. He worked with Fiona Carlton. I don't know why they were meeting in a hotel, but I'm willing to bet it wasn't to do the nasty, considering she was only in there for fifteen minutes. Unless he's a quick worker.'

Harry's phone rang and he stepped into his office to take the call.

'Harry, it's Kate from the mortuary. We were going over Fiona Carlton's body since they violated it, and we took photos of the mark on her head where she was struck. It looks like an eye.'

EIGHTEEN

'What do you think of the new sergeant?' Harry said as Alex drove them back to the Bush Estate. It was damp and miserable, a grey sky threatening to dump its contents on them as they pulled into the car park.

Harry heard a buzzing above them and looked up to the sky. He saw the little flashing lights.

'Look, there's a drone,' he said. Alex turned to look up at it.

'Nothing unusual about those nowadays. Arseholes are always flying them about.'

'It's like it's watching us. Probably McCallum got a bit bored playing with his toy cars and he's moved onto his wee aeroplanes,' Alex said.

Inside, they were shown into a waiting area. And then James McCallum appeared, followed by a woman who the detectives hadn't seen before.

'Good morning! And how can I be of help today?' He smiled at them, and Harry couldn't be sure if this was the man's normal personality or whether he'd had too much caffeine that morning.

'We'd like to talk with Dave Pierce, one of your employees.'

'Dave Pierce? I don't know him personally, but we do have a lot of employees. I'll have somebody find him for you. May I ask what's it in connection with?'

'I'm sorry, I can't discuss that. It's a question of privacy.'

'No problem.' The smile stayed fixed. 'Give me five minutes and I'll see what I can do. Let's go and have a coffee while we see if this Mr Pierce is indeed a member of my staff.'

They got in the lift and stepped off at the basement level. The young woman stayed in the lift and it took her away again. 'Denise will do the searching. She has plenty of people working under her. Come on, I want to show you some other stuff. How did you like the cars?'

They were going along a white corridor, approaching a security station.

'It was impressive,' Harry said.

'And you, Miss Maxwell?'

'Cars are a means of getting from point A to point B.'

'Exactly!' he said, beaming a smile at her. 'And don't we all want to get there safely?'

'Of course we do. I think we need to educate young drivers though, not rely on computers.'

Harry looked at her like she had just insulted the Queen.

McCallum merely laughed. 'I can sense some scepticism.' They approached the security guards. 'These are police officers. Let us through, please.'

'Yes, sir.'

Two glass doors ahead of them slid open and McCallum wheeled his chair through, followed by the detectives. The made their way down another corridor before turning left, then they were into a lab of sorts, with giant screens and consoles and a large crowd of people working.

'This is the lab where we work on large vehicles. It's not just cars that will be self-driving. You may have seen the YouTube video of Mercedes Benz putting their large articulated truck through its paces on a private track? Very impressive. We have our own version. Fitted with computers that interact with not just other cars and vans, but with their surroundings. And yes, nowadays, cars are fitted with pedestrian detection software, and that is the next step in automation, but we take that several steps further.'

He rolled over to a set of large windows and Harry

stood beside him. They looked into an arena that must have been the size of ten football fields.

'That's massive,' he said.

'There's train tunnels at both ends. See them?'

'Yes.'

'Two adjacent at either end. The train runs in a loop. We can watch it from here and there are also large screens that provide an alternative view.'

McCallum looked over to one of the techs. 'Bring the train in.' Then he turned back to the window and he and Harry looked down. Alex stood beside Harry.

'Who are those people down there?' she asked.

McCallum was sitting in front of a console and he typed some instructions. The window in front of him became a TV screen and he used a joystick to zoom down.

'Jesus,' Alex said.

'Not quite. They're automatons. More commonly known as robots. We're ninety-nine per cent sure that they're in a safe environment, but it's that one percent that could make the difference, so we're not using humans just now.'

He zoomed out a bit and they saw the lights of a train coming out of the tunnel. Harry looked over and saw a man sitting in what looked like a gaming chair, a huge console in front of him. The train driver. The screen in front of the man showed a simulated view out of the train window.

On another console, a man sat inside a tipper truck.

'Let me switch on the audio, so we can hear things better.' He looked at Alex. 'So you can hear the robots screaming.'

Alex looked at him like he was insane.

'I'm kidding,' he said. 'Listen to the silence.'

They couldn't hear anything but a low hum.

'We have to artificially dial some noise in, just so people can hear the traffic. You wouldn't believe how quiet we've made these electric engines.'

He played around with a few sliders on the console and they could start to hear engine noises.

McCallum smiled, obviously enjoying himself. 'People are used to hearing diesel engines, so we fit the trucks with a diesel engine sound. Thankfully, not the emissions just the noise.'

A tipper truck came into view. Harry turned to look over at the train cab and saw it was in the tunnel. A large speedometer in the top right-hand corner read that the train was travelling at forty miles an hour.

The tipper approached a level crossing and drove onto the tracks and stopped.

'We do real-world scenarios here. I've watched trucks getting stuck on level crossings. What if suddenly the tipper lost power for some reason? Now he's on the crossing and the barriers are coming down. The train is going to collide with the truck. Only it isn't.'

They could see a red beacon flashing on the roof of the truck.

'That's it just pointing out its position and letting us know which vehicle is in play. It's more a visual thing for any guests we have watching. But the truck is already communicating with the train, through its own Wi-Fi. A box at the side of the barriers is sending out the signal that a train is approaching and the truck has picked up the signal. The truck is talking with the box, telling it that it has a problem and is now blocking the tracks. The box is talking to the train and an emergency procedure has been put in place. The train is now braking. By the time the gates come down, a sweep is made of the track, it's been calculated that the train will have enough time to stop because of the speed limit on the approach to the crossing. The train knows what the speed limit is, so there's no human input. If a driver is distracted on a normal train, the train can speed up and be doing way over the speed limit. This system takes the need for humans out of the equation.'

'What if some idiot drives round the barrier?' Alex said.

'As you can see, the barriers cover the whole road.

And we're talking about a time when all the idiots will, in effect, be just passengers. The vehicles are making all of the decisions.'

Harry watched the train come out of the tunnel and slow down and stop before it got to the truck.

'One day, nobody will be killed in a vehicle on a level crossing.'

'I can only imagine how much money that will cost,' Alex said.

'The savings will be made by not having to buy fuel. The engines on the train and truck are self-generating electric engines. They don't need recharging stations. They are highly advanced and very expensive, but the cost will come down. Right now, we obviously have more affordable electric vehicles that need charging, but what you see there is the future.'

'Way in the future, I would imagine,' Harry said.

'Think back twenty years, Chief Inspector; mobile phones were in their infancy. New technology, just becoming more widespread. Now think back thirty, forty years. What were mobile phones like back then? Big bricks with a handset on top. Compare the two. The former, only people with money could have one. How many young people do you know who don't have a phone? And it fits in their pocket! In thirty years, we'll be travelling around in electric cars that will be powering themselves and the greedy oil company execs will be crying in their soup. They've had it their own way for too long, poisoning the planet with their fuels and plastics. The planet can be saved, Harry, but we all need to be on board. And my company will be leading the way.'

'Zero emissions,' Alex said.

'Exactly. But we need the AI to go along with this. Human interaction will need to be at a minimum. Not taken out of the picture entirely, but at a minimum. At McCallum Technology we're staying two steps ahead. The world isn't ready for this technology at the moment, but when they are, we will be at the forefront. Meantime, our self-driving cars are almost ready to be unleashed onto the world, and when we have finished testing the retro-fit units, there will be nothing stopping us. The world will be a safer, and cleaner place! And you never know, maybe somebody will invent a plastic bottle that degrades in weeks, not centuries.'

'We can hope,' Harry said, feeling that Alex was about to go on a rant.

'Come on then, let's find that coffee. We have a nice lounge upstairs.' He led them back out and when they got to the lounge, which was really a canteen with comfortable seats, the assistant came to them.

'We do have a Dave Pierce who works for us. He was due to be at work right now, but there's no sign of him. He's a no-call, no-show.'

'Really?' McCallum said, clearly annoyed. 'What department does he work in?'

'He's a programmer, sir.'

'That's not good enough. Does he have a habit of this?'

'No, sir. First time.'

'Can we have his address?' Harry asked.

'Of course.' McCallum nodded to the woman, who brought out a piece of paper with Pierce's address on it.

'Thank you.' Harry and Alex stood up. 'Is your wife not around today?'

The question threw McCallum for a second but he smiled quickly. 'She's in a meeting with some shareholders. Why? Did you want to have a talk with her?'

'Oh, no, I was just wondering. Thank you for your time, Mr McCallum.'

'Please come around anytime.'

Outside, the drone was nowhere to be seen.

But Max Blue was standing at a window on the top level of the house.

Watching them. He smiled then turned away.

'That was an eye-opener,' Harry said as Alex drove away in the Honda.

'Boys and their toys, eh? I could see you starting to foam at the mouth.'

'I have to admit, if that stuff becomes reality, it could save a lot of lives. How many times have we read about vehicles being stuck on a level crossing? Not just here, but in America. All over the world. And that's not taking into account the environment.'

'I didn't see you as being an environmentalist.'

'It's not that, Alex, it just pisses me off that people with money are ruining the planet that belongs to us all, while they're still getting rich. We all need to be more proactive, and I haven't seen a rich man be more proactive when it comes to the environment than McCallum.'

'His business is AI, and if you want my honest opinion, his first consideration isn't the environment. But his machines will be good for the future, which is a good thing.'

'I don't disagree. But let's not lose focus of why we're here in the first place.'

'I know. Dave Pierce might be a killer.'

She drove Harry's car onto Bush Loan Road, turning left, and then the car accelerated.

'Whoa there, Stirling Moss.'

'Fuck, Harry, it's not me!' Alex screamed. The car took off faster and she wrestled with the controls. 'My foot's on the fucking brake but it's not stopping!'

They were onto a straight part of the road but a slight curve to the left was coming up and the car was already doing sixty and getting faster. She guided the car and then there was a slight curve to the right and then the A702 main road into Edinburgh was only a few hundred yards ahead.

'Turn the ignition key!' Harry shouted. 'Put it in neutral!'

Alex did both things and then the car started to slow down and came to an exact stop at the T-junction.

'Jesus Christ, what the hell just happened?' Harry said, looking at Alex, who was visibly shaken.

Then they saw the tendril of smoke creeping out from under the bonnet of the car. They both jumped out just as the flames started licking out from under it.

They got out of the way and as Harry took out his phone and made the call, Alex looked up into the air.

And saw the drone watching them before it flew away.

NINETEEN

Dave Pierce was exhausted. Every night now, sleep eluded him. He couldn't concentrate at work.

Especially after what had happened to Fiona.

Two women he knew, both dying in the space of a few months. He didn't like that at all, and it gave him a bad feeling. He was thinking of moving on, starting afresh.

Besides, what was left here for him? Nothing. He'd started to hate his job, his girlfriend was dead, and there was no prospect of advancement with McCallum. Things couldn't get any worse, he thought, then the doorbell rang. Things were about to get a *lot* worse.

'Oh, it's you, he said to the visitor. 'What brings you here?'

'Are you going to leave me standing on your doorstep?'

Pierce stood for a moment, not wanting to let the man in. 'I'm busy.'

'This won't take long.'

'Famous last words.'

'I have something for you.'

'What?'

The man grinned. 'What you've been up to lately, and you want to discuss it with me at your front door?'

'I don't know what you're talking about.'

'I think you do.' He held up a flash drive.

'What's on that?'

'Again, walls have ears. Do you really expect me to stand out on your landing and talk about what's been going on?'

Pierce ran his tongue over his lips which were starting to dry out. 'You'd better come in.'

'That's more like it.'

Pierce closed the door behind them as the man walked up the hall. He'd been here before. Knew the layout of the flat.

'How about a cup of tea?' he said.

'I'm not a café,' Pierce answered, brushing past the man. He went into his little office. It was a box room, which was a fancier way of saying it was a large cupboard with a window.

'Can I have a drink of water? I'm parched.'

'Help yourself. You know where the kitchen is.'

He heard the man go through and then the tap was running for a few seconds. He pressed the on button and waited for the computer to come to life.

The man came back.

Pierce sat himself down at his computer. 'I'm assuming you want me to plug the flash drive in?'

'That would be helpful. You can see for yourself what's on it.'

Pierce let out a sigh, not making any effort to disguise it. He took the flash drive and plugged it into the tower that sat next to the monitor.

He opened it up and looked at the images. 'What the fuck is this?' he said, and had just started turning round when he felt the blinding pain in his head. Then again on the top of his head. The man tried for a third time, but Pierce dodged it. Then the man grabbed his hair and pulled him off the chair and dragged him kicking and yelling across to his bedroom.

The man roughly threw Pierce onto his bed then pulled the kitchen knife out of his pocket. It was a steak knife, Pierce realised, just before it was plunged into his chest, over and over.

The man walked back to the box room and retrieved his flash drive.

And calmly walked out.

TWENTY

'You were lucky you could stop the car in time,' the fire commander said as the last of the smoke fizzled out. The day had gotten colder but they'd warmed up a little from the flames of the car on fire.

'Bloody thing wouldn't stop,' Harry said.

'It could be an electrical fault. Something burning through and then the brakes don't get the message.'

DI Karen Shiels turned up with Simon Gregg shortly afterwards.

'Jesus, boss, is everything okay?' she asked.

Harry told them what happened.

She looked shocked. 'I read a news article about something like this happening to a car somewhere in America; some computer geek was able to hack into a car's computer system and he took it over. He could steer it, do anything he wanted because he hijacked the car's computer system.'

'I don't think my wife's old Honda would have a sophisticated computer system. Nobody could hack into it, I don't think.'

'Unless they put in a retrofit box that brought the car's brain bang up to date,' Alex said.

'Why would anybody do that?'

'Why would somebody kill Fiona Carlton?'

He didn't have that answer. 'Where's the new girl?'

'Back in the office. She's looking over the schematics that were on the flash drive and the computer, see if she can see anything that we missed.'

'Ricky, the tech guy, said he couldn't see anything that sticks out. They both have schematics on them, but if you were to try and fit one thing in with another, they wouldn't join up.'

He pulled up his collar against the chill wind that was coming off the Pentlands and they sat in the car until the breakdown truck came for what was left of Harry's car.

'I hope you didn't have a sentimental attachment to her,' Alex said as they watched the truck and the fire engines pull away.

'It wasn't mine. So no, I don't have any attachment to it.'

'This is just the perfect excuse to get a Beemer like me.'

'I have to admit I've never had so many beamers since I met you.'

'Now you're just being ridiculous. In front of the DI as well.'

Karen smiled. 'Just wait 'til he has a sesh with us. I'm sure there will be more than a few beamers that night.'

'And that's just watching me dance.' Harry sat in the front passenger seat as Karen drove them back into town. Down to Harrison Road, Dave Pierce's address.

It was a flat in a tenement, one of the older buildings.

'He was a no-call, no-show at work this morning,' Harry said as they went up one flight to the number they had been given at McCallum Technology.

'This is the man who was running from our victim, so keep your eyes peeled. He might be a fighter with a knife.'

The others took out their extendable batons, like they were part of a circus act. Harry rang the bell and banged on the door. 'Police! Open up!'

A neighbour across the way opened her door. 'Is everything alright?'

'Have you seen Mr Pierce?' Alex asked her.

'No, I'm sorry. Not since last night when he was

going out. I was coming in. Is there anything I can help you with?'

'Just stand back, ma'am,' Karen said.

Harry nodded to Gregg. 'Get that door in, son, I smell something funny.'

Gregg lifted a leg when the woman stopped him. 'I have a key, if that helps?'

Gregg stopped with his leg up, and they looked at the woman.

'That would be great,' Harry said, and they watched her scuttle away.

'Nice yoga move,' Alex said.

'It's a Kung Fu move,' he replied.

'From a cartoon?' Harry said. 'Put your leg down, silly sod.'

The woman came back with the key, and whilst not quite asking if she could stay and watch, she pulled her cardigan tighter round herself, implying that she was in this for the long haul.

'You want me to go in first?' Gregg said.

Harry handed him the key. 'No point in having a dog and barking yourself, is there?'

DC Simon Gregg had never backed down from a fight in his life but wasn't stupid. He knew how to fight with his baton and would not hesitate for a moment to use it. Harry let Karen and Alex follow him in while he guarded their backs.

They cleared each room, leaving the bedroom until last.

Gregg didn't hesitate and went in first.

Dave Pierce was waiting for them, or rather his lifeless corpse was. His eyes were looking at them, pleading for help that had arrived too late. A kitchen knife was sticking out of his chest, his shirt stained a dark red. His face had marks on it from being beaten with a blunt object.

Each of the detectives had smelled death before, but it was never something they got used to.

Karen Shiels backed out, getting on her radio without being asked to.

'Jesus, that's fuckin boggin,' Gregg said. 'This reminds me of the time I was in uniform and we found an old boy in his house. Been dead for weeks and his two dugs had started eating him. That was fuckin minging.'

'Well, thanks for that trip down memory lane. Not that I wanted any dinner tonight,' Harry said. 'Two dugs indeed.'

'You should have been there.'

'Why? We have you to tell us all about it in great detail.' He shook his head and turned to Alex. 'This is the third person connected to McCallum Technology who's died.'

'Who's the third one?'

'Bea Anderson.'

'I thought they said she *didn't* work there.'

'They did. I think whoever killed her made a mistake. He was after Maggie Carlton, and he thought he'd killed her but he'd killed Bea because she was in Maggie's house looking for something.'

'She just happened to be in there while there was a lunatic killer waiting?' She sounded sceptical.

'No, I think the killer turned up to do in Maggie, and Bea was creeping about in the dark, and he *thought* it was Maggie, because Maggie was his target.'

'That means she's still in danger.'

'I wonder if there are other people on his list?' Alex said. 'And why target this small group of friends?'

They left the bedroom to wait on the cavalry turning up. They pulled on nitrile gloves and started looking around the flat. Nothing remarkable stood out. Pierce had kept the place clean. The décor was fresh. Harry walked into the little box room where the computer desk sat. There was a window high up on the wall, giving plenty of light. The computer tower had its power light on, and when Harry nudged the desk with his thigh, the monitor sprang into life.

He sat on the chair, not sure if forensics would have been able to pull anything from the vinyl covering. He rolled the mouse around on its mat, and clicked on the icon that showed something was minimised.

Up came an article about James McCallum and his quest to be one of the first companies in the world to run electric vehicles. Harry started reading, scrolling down the article, which wasn't akin to watching paint dry like he had thought it would be.

A lot of the stuff mentioned was what he, Harry, had been given a demonstration of at the Bush facility. But it was mention of something else that caught his eye.

McCallum was working on a military contract. It didn't go into exact details, but it was widely known that McCallum Technology was working with the British government.

He minimised the page and was about to roll the chair back when he noticed the wallpaper Pierce had put on his desktop; it was a photo of himself, his face close to a young woman.

Linda Smith.

'Hey, Alex,' he shouted.

She came through to him. 'What you got?'

'Doesn't that look like Linda Smith?' he said, pointing to the screen.

Alex bent a little closer. 'From what I remember of her. There was a similar photo on a sideboard in her dad's house.'

Harry took his phone out and snapped a photo of the screen.

'Let's go for a drive.'

'We don't have a car, remember? Honey the Happy Honda went to that great scrapyard in the sky.'

'I won't dignify that with an answer.'

Karen Shiels came back in.

'Karen, can you and Gregg hold the fort here while me and Alex go and visit somebody? I'll need the car keys. Have Eve Bell come up with another pool car.'

'Sure, no bother.' She handed him the car keys.

'If Gregg asks if you want to hear a story about two wee dugs, taser him.'

TWENTY-ONE

'That was a fucking stupid idea of yours,' Melissa McCallum said, pacing around the hotel room. 'They're police officers for God's sake.'

'Don't wet your panties,' Max Blue said, then immediately regretted it when she flew at him.

'Don't you ever fucking talk to me like that!' she yelled.

'Okay, I'm sorry. I'm just on edge.' He looked into her eyes and only saw two, deep pits that were a conduit to hell itself.

Her breathing was coming fast, her body going into *fight* mode without the slightest thought of whether it should go into *flight* mode. Blue knew she had a temper but lately, he was seeing it in action.

'Just relax. Everything is going smoothly.'

'That's just the thing. I can't relax. The contract is

coming up for final revision, so the timing is crucial, you know that.'

'Everything's in place.' Blue was starting to feel edgy. 'What about the other sister?' he asked, putting ice into the glass.

'Hopefully she'll give up the witch hunt soon. Or else we might have to scare her.'

Her mobile phone rang and she fished it out of her pocket. 'Yes?'

'Where are you?'

'I'm shopping. Why?' She knew her voice sounded sharp, but her husband was used to it.

'We have a problem. One of our programmers was found dead. Dave Pierce.'

'How is that our problem?'

'Don't you think they're going to wonder why two of our employees are dead?'

'I couldn't care less.'

'He was the one who was working with Fiona Carlton, Melissa.'

'I don't see what that's got to do with us.'

James McCallum hung up.

'Who was that?' Blue said, not liking the look on her face.

'Dave Pierce was found dead.'

'Jesus. How the hell did that happen?'

She ran a hand through her hair. The hotel room

was starting to feel stifling. 'I don't fucking know. He was a careless bastard. And now he's dead.'

'We just have to keep it together for a little while longer, then everything will fall into place.'

She looked up at him. 'Then we can be together. Just you and I.'

'It's going to work out,' he assured her.

'Just call your people. And make sure they don't get the jitters if they find out about the dead man.'

He would call them alright. And everything he'd said was the truth; it *was* going to be alright.

For him.

TWENTY-TWO

'Look on the bright side, the garage who are doing up your car might get the job done quicker now that you're carless,' Alex said as she drove the manky old Vauxhall up Harrison Road towards Colinton Road.

'Classic cars take time. They can't be rushed.'

'I said that to see if you would tell me the truth or maintain the fairy tale you have going.'

'I may have to get myself a newer runabout while I'm waiting for the classic to be finished.'

'Daft *and* delusional. Qualities that can only be attributed to senior officers.'

'Which you will not get to be if you keep this pish up.'

'You could always buy an old pool car like this when they sell them.'

'I was thinking about a quality piece of engineering.'

'Like Betty?' she said, grinning.

'Not quite.'

'Tiny the Toyota, more like, eh?' She shook her head in disgust as she turned into the street they were looking for in Glenlockhart.

'Now, try and turn your attention to the murder case we're working instead of some children's show where all the vehicles have names.'

'Aye aye, Captain.' She parked in front of the bungalow and walked up to the front door, Harry looking around.

Brian Smith answered the door, scowling when he saw who it was. 'Help you?' he said, leaning heavily on his walking stick. It was one of the metal, NHS-issue kind. Loved by benefits cheats everywhere, Harry thought.

'We'd like a word, Mr Smith, if you don't mind.'

'Unless you've come to tell me you've caught my daughter's killer, I do mind.'

'I don't have any news on that front,' Harry said.

Smith stepped back slightly, as if he was about to shut the front door.

'I wanted to ask you about Dave Pierce.'

Smith stopped. 'What about him?'

'He *was* your daughter's boyfriend, wasn't he?'

JOHN CARSON

He looked between Harry and Alex before answering. 'Yes, he was. He was her boyfriend at the time of her death. Useless bastard if ever I met one.'

'Why do you say that?' Alex said, shrugging her coat up further. It was clear that Smith wasn't going to invite them in for tea and crumpets.

'He should have been protecting my daughter, that's why!' Smith stopped short of adding *you silly cow* to the end of his sentence, but the implication was there.

'She was a trained police officer, why would she need protecting?' Harry said, starting to get irritated.

'He was her boyfriend. He was supposed to look after her. I mean, it's not as if I could!' He shook his walking stick. 'I could when she was little, but not now. Not after the accident. That's where a father steps aside and lets the boyfriend take over. But that useless sod had his head in a computer all the time. Linda was the fighter, not him.'

'He's dead,' Harry said.

Smith stopped talking and looked at Harry. 'What? How?'

'We're still determining the cause.'

'Oh. I wonder what's happened?'

'Did you keep in touch with him after Linda's death?' Alex asked.

'No. I didn't see him after the funeral. I asked him

for some of her stuff, but he kept what was at her house. He wanted to keep it himself.'

'Do you know if he had any problems with anybody?' Harry said.

'Not that I know of, but he was an obnoxious prick.' He looked at his watch. 'As much as I'd like to stay and chat...'

'We'll leave you to it—' But Smith had already closed the door. They walked back to the car and Harry turned to look at the bungalow. 'I've seen some people mourning, but he takes the biscuit.'

'He's certainly a strange one.'

They drove down the road. 'I'll have to go along and have my tyres blown up,' Alex said.

Harry looked at his watch. As usual, the day had got away from them and darkness was slowly covering the city with its blanket.

'Take that big lump of wood with you.'

Alex raised her eyebrows at him.

'You know I mean Gregg. Just don't go alone.'

'Lump of wood? I thought you would have called him *that lanky streak of piss.*'

'I'm graduating up to that.' He called Karen Shiels. There wasn't anything more they could do at the crime scene as forensics had turned up and kicked everybody out.

'The mortuary crowd have turned up and they're

waiting to take him away,' Karen added, making it sound like the mortuary crowd were some sort of rabble.

'Get Gregg to go back with Alex to her house. She needs her tyres blown up and he's full of air.'

Silence for a moment.

'No, really, Karen, I need him to go with her, just to watch her back.'

'Okay, sir. I'm at the office. I'll get Gregg to get a pool car.'

'No need, Karen. Alex is going to drop me off then she'll pick up Gregg.'

'I'll get him to wait outside.'

He hung up and Alex reached his house a few minutes later.

'Don't go talking to any strangers,' he said. 'See you back home.'

'Whatever you say, boss.'

He hated to admit it, but it was good having Alex stay with him for a little while. Not that he got bored, but it was another human to talk to. He had thought about getting a cat, but it meant remembering to feed it. And clean up after it. At least Alex cleaned up after herself.

He watched her pull away and then stood at his stair door, contemplating whether to go round to Vanessa's. He walked to the end of the street, pulling his collar up. He felt much colder after the heat of the car.

He stood by the hedge that bordered the bowling club and looked up Learnmonth Place, towards Vanessa's house. He thought about the first time he'd been in there, how warm and inviting it had been. Christ, that was almost two years ago now.

He knew she was playing games with him, but he couldn't completely let go of the good times they'd had. And still could have had, Harry, he thought. Why couldn't she have just wanted things to go on the way they were? He started walking up the hill a bit then stopped. What was he doing? Making things worse for himself. She would think he was weak, and then the games really would start.

He turned back and walked back to his door. Inside, he climbed to the top floor and was about to turn the key in the lock when his neighbour across the way opened her door.

'There you are, Harry,' she said, smiling at him. She was a young woman, not long moved in. 'Your girl-friend asked me to give you this.'

'What is it?'

'A big brown envelope. What does it look like to you?' She laughed as she handed it over to him and stepped back inside her own flat.

'Thanks, Mia.'

She gave a little wave before closing the door all the way. He looked at the envelope; it was sealed and had his name written on the front.

What was Vanessa doing now? Maybe he had been right not to go up to her house.

He let himself in and put some lights on and switched the kettle on, then thought better of it and took a bottle of beer from the fridge. He took his jacket off and hung it up, then sat down on the settee in the living room and tore the envelope open.

Inside was a newspaper article.

He scanned it, looking at the photos. It was about a helicopter that had crashed a few months earlier, in the Highlands. It had been foggy, and the helicopter had crashed into some woods, killing everybody on board.

He put the article and envelope down on the coffee table and went out and across to his neighbour. She answered after a few minutes.

'Hey, Mia, did you ever see my girlfriend Vanessa up here?'

She looked at him, her smile fading a bit. 'I don't think so. I'm not sure. If I did, you never introduced me to her.'

'You said my girlfriend dropped that envelope off. What did she look like? Got a few spare pounds on her, brown hair.' *Lies a lot.*

She giggled. 'Who says that about a woman? A few extra pounds. I hope you don't say that about me!'

Mia was the exact opposite of Vanessa. If she turned sideways beside a lamppost, she'd disappear. 'Of course not.'

'Well, she was young, blonde, about my height and not skinny, but not heavy either.'

'Sounds like my dream woman, but unfortunately she isn't my girlfriend. I don't suppose she left a name?'

'No. She just said, could you please give this to Harry?'

'Thank you.'

Mia was about to close her front door when Harry stopped her. 'Just one more thing; I don't suppose you saw her get into a car?'

'Well, Harry, you know I'm not a nosy cow or anything, but I did think it was a bit strange, her asking me to give you this when she could have put it through your letterbox, so I did look out and she stood at the side of the road. Then a big, black car came along and picked her up.'

'Do you know what kind of car it was?'

'One of those big things. The kind you see rich country folk and snobby mothers dropping their kids off at school in.'

'A Range Rover?'

'Yes!' she exclaimed, pointing her finger at him, like

he had just won first prize in a competition only she knew about.

Harry thanked her and went back into his own flat. He drank some of the beer and started reading through the article again.

And one name jumped out at him.

TWENTY-THREE

'Nice street,' DC Simon Gregg said, stopping the car at the entrance. It was narrow and there didn't appear to be any parking spaces further down.

'I like it.'

'Look, I'll park on the main street around the corner then I'll walk round.'

'You don't have to, Simon. I'll be fine. Harry was just exaggerating. You can go home.'

'Like hell I will. Just sit tight and we'll have you up and running soon.' He backed out and he found a space outside what used to be little shops but had long ago been converted to flats.

They started walking round, darkness enveloping the city now.

'What do you think of McNeil?' Gregg asked.

'I like him. I really do. He's fair and he's not worried about getting his hands dirty. He'll roll his sleeves up and get in about somebody.' They turned the corner into her street. 'Why? What do you think of him?'

He grinned. 'He busts my balls all the time, but I like him a lot. Better than that wanker Stan Weaver. I get the feeling that when the shit goes down, McNeil will have our backs.'

They walked down towards Alex's BMW and she stopped.

'What's wrong?' Gregg asked.

'Look. The tyres. They're inflated.'

'What? I thought you said they were all flat?'

'They were.'

'Are you sure, Alex? It was dark that night.'

She turned to look at him. 'I'm not dumb, Simon. Ask Harry. About the tyres, I mean.'

'If you say so.'

'I do say so. What the hell?' She shook her head.

'Maybe they self-inflate.'

She looked at him. 'I am at a total loss for words right now. Self-inflate? Does that come with the self-cleaning package? And the self-hoovering package.'

Gregg shrugged. 'I don't know.'

'For God's sake.'

'I don't know much about cars, you know that.'

'I know that, but you can have an intelligent guess sometimes.'

'I don't know what to tell you. Maybe a neighbour who thinks he's in with a chance with you?'

'Shut up. They're all older and married. I think I'm the youngest on the street.'

'Don't look a gift horse, and all that.' He smiled at her. 'You going to be okay?'

'Of course. I just need to go in and get my car keys. Thanks for driving me.'

'No problem. I might be as dumb as an ox, but if somebody lifted his hand to you, I'd break him into little pieces.'

'I know you would.' She patted his arm.

He insisted he go into the house to make sure it was clear, but she was right behind him. It was empty.

'See you at work tomorrow.'

'See you, big guy.' She watched him walk down the stairs and walk up the road heading back to the car, and wondered if he got lonely and still mourned the loss of his wife and baby girl.

She grabbed her car keys and went down to the little BMW. It felt good to get in behind the wheel after driving the pool car. She felt good going back to Harry's flat. He was her boss, but she also regarded him as a friend now. She had lost a lot of her friends after becoming a copper, and now she spent her time hanging out occasionally with some other female coppers.

She was glad Angie Patterson had decided to come down from the Highlands to live in Edinburgh. Angie liked Harry a lot, but Alex didn't know if the two of them would hit it off enough to start going out.

She started the car and drove it slowly out of her street, turning right. She would have to go round by Inverleith Park since the council had decided in their wisdom to close St Bernard's Row to through traffic. Sometimes she wondered about the sense in blocking off rat runs, just so the traffic can sit in other streets, spewing their fumes into the air.

She turned up Arboretum Avenue, following the road round, her bright headlight beams cutting through the darkness. She started to slow down at the top of the road as she approached the T-junction with Inverleith Terrace and then the car started speeding up. She jammed her foot on the brakes, but nothing. She tried to steer the car to the side of the road but her input did nothing. The car flew across the traffic island, knocking down an illuminated traffic sign, and the car careened across the road onto the opposite side and smashed into the front of a parked car, throwing her against the steering wheel.

The airbags exploded and she felt herself being held back by the seatbelt as her face smashed into the airbag.

The car crumpled at the front with a loud explosion. As she settled back into her seat, she saw the first wisps of smoke snaking up from the front of the car in the dark.

She was aware of other vehicles stopping. She felt the first tendrils of panic as she grabbed the handle to open the door and it wouldn't open. She pulled and pulled but nothing happened.

That's when all her training went out the window. She tried undoing her seatbelt but it was stuck. And that's when her panic went into overdrive.

There were lights outside, vehicles stopping, people shouting. Then she saw a shadow at her door. She couldn't see for the smoke in front of her windscreen, but the man had jumped out of his car and tried to put out the fire with an extinguisher.

Then he was banging on the glass. He was screaming at her. *Duck!*

She leant sideways further into the car and he banged on the glass with the red extinguisher until the glass shattered. He threw the extinguisher aside and then reached in with a knife and cut her belt. She sat up and scrambled to get out and the man's hands grabbed her and pulled her free.

She fell on the pavement, gasping and crying. Then she looked up into the dark night sky, and saw the little green and red lights.

And heard the buzzing as the drone flew away.

TWENTY-FOUR

Harry parked the pool car in the car park in the Royal Infirmary in Little France. Inside, he was taken right to the bay where Alex was. She smiled when he came in.

'Thank God you're alright,' he said. He held her hand for a second.

'I'm more shook up than anything else. A few cuts and scrapes and I jarred my shoulder, but I'll be fine.'

The doctor came in. 'She was lucky,' he said after Harry identified himself. 'A few days rest and painkillers and she'll be right as rain. She can go home now. Follow up with your doctor.'

'Jesus, I nearly crapped myself when I got a call from control. What happened?'

'I couldn't control the car, Harry. Just like your car when I was driving today. I had no input. Some bastard took it over.'

'How? How could they do that?'

'I don't know how, but when me and Simon got to the car, the tyres had been inflated. I thought it strange, but then I thought maybe one of my neighbours had done it for me. I got in and drove away and when I got near Inverleith Park, the car got away from me.'

'It was hijacked,' Harry said, gritting his teeth.

She nodded. 'Thank God that guy pulled me out.'

'Did you get his name? As a witness.'

'No. I was busy lying on the ground watching the little drone fly away.'

'What? A fucking drone? Well, guess who we'll be talking to tomorrow. I'll kick his fucking arse, trying that on with us. And you, twice in one day. That's attempted murder.'

'They'll cover their backs, and you know it. We have to find out why they want to harm us.'

A nurse came in with the discharge papers. 'You can go home. Take more painkillers before bed. Is this your husband?'

Harry didn't say anything for a second.

'No, he's my boss,' Alex said, trying to keep a straight face. 'We're both police officers.'

'Oh, right. Do you have anybody at home to look after you, if you feel you need to come back here?' the older woman asked.

'Yes. I'm staying with a good friend of mine.'

'Good. You can leave when you're ready.'

Alex had blood down the front of her shirt from her busted nose. 'It isn't broken, thank God, but it's going to hurt for a week or more.'

'We'll get you cleaned up. You hungry? I have the car outside. I've called Jeni Bridge and updated her on the situation. She's livid. We can—'

'Ease up there, Harry. My face will be sore, but Betty protected me like she should have. I can't fault the BMW but somebody tampered with her. But she's ruined now.'

'She was burnt out. Just like my... I mean, my ex's Honda.'

She laughed. 'Christ, don't make me laugh. My ribs feel like they've been kicked. And yes, I feel hungry. Maybe hit the chippie on the way home? You can drop me off at my place. I think I'll be safe.'

'Safe? You've been involved in two accidents in one day. There's no way you're going to stay at your place. I mean, if that's okay with you.'

'It is. And thanks for caring.'

'I would do it for any of my officers.'

'I know you would. But thank you anyway.'

They started walking out together. 'I've had your car taken to the impound yard. They'll have some techs look it over. Or what's left of it.'

'They won't find anything. Just like they won't find

anything on your car. Whatever it was they put in there, the fire will have taken care of it.'

'Let's just get you back to my place and get you into something more comfortable.'

'Is that your best pick-up line?'

'Nope. My best pick-up line is, *I'm Harry. You're welcome.*' He grinned at her.

'It would work on me.'

'Of course it would. You're vulnerable. You let somebody sell you a BMW.'

'My new car has to be a Honda CR-V.'

'Or a manky old Vauxhall. One of which I just happen to have out here.'

She shivered in the cold until they got across to the car.

'There is something I want to mention,' Alex said as they got into the Vauxhall.

'What's that?'

'The bloke who pulled me out of the car and probably saved my life.'

'What about him?'

'He was driving a Range Rover. It was the guy we saw in the pub the other night.'

TWENTY-FIVE

'You did what? You stupid bastard. What are you trying to do? Bring us all down?' Melissa McCallum paced back and forward in her office.

Max Blue stood in front of her, smiling. Like he was enjoying this.

'You need to relax more. You're too tense. Here, let Maxi take care of you.' He stepped towards her.

'Fuck off. Get away from me. Playing with fucking drones. God almighty, what if you'd killed her? What if you'd killed them both earlier today?'

Blue was still smiling, like he couldn't help himself. 'That was our technology working perfectly. The car accelerated because I made it, then I switched it into auto mode and it stopped perfectly. Then tonight, with the other one, it went exactly where I told it to go. You have to believe in your own products, Melissa.'

She stopped and looked at him. 'They're police officers. You might have a complete disregard for the law where you come from, but here, they will hunt you down and rip you a new arsehole. Oh yes, the courts are about as useful as a chocolate fireguard, but the police tend to look after their own. You would die in custody after falling down some stairs accidentally.'

'God, look at you. I don't think I could be turned on any more than I am now.'

'Jesus Christ. Will you listen to yourself? Get a fucking grip. Tomorrow is when the world sees what McCallum Technology is all about and we don't need any unwanted attention.'

Blue was still smiling like a schoolboy who didn't know he was in trouble.

'I just wanted that McNeil guy to be occupied with something other than bugging us.'

Melissa lowered her head and shook it. Then she locked eyes with him. 'Don't you see? By doing what you did with that bloody drone, you have done just the opposite. Now they're going to be all over us.'

'Somebody pulled her from the car. That wasn't supposed to happen.'

'Oh my God. You were actually trying to kill her?'

'I assumed she would be able to get out of the car on her own without any help.'

'Oh don't fucking lie.'

Blue wasn't fazed. 'Don't get all sanctimonious on me now. This is just a means to an end. Besides, if I'd wanted to kill her, I would have waited until she was on that long street and taken the car up to a hundred. But I didn't.'

'Oh, I should feel grateful for that?'

Blue laughed. 'Yes.'

'This is not funny, Max. The investors' reps are coming tomorrow and everything has to go according to plan. We cannot afford to have anything come back at us.'

He walked over and held her. 'Don't worry, it won't.'

'I hope not, Max. We've come this far.'

'Listen, I was with the engineers all day today, going over last-minute calibrations. I was working on the software. It's going perfectly.'

'Good. By this time tomorrow, we'll be on our way. And nothing will stop us.'

TWENTY-SIX

Harry walked round to the passenger side to grab the fish suppers.

'How you feeling now?' he asked.

'Harry, between the chippie and here, I haven't deteriorated. I'm fine. You don't have to act like a mother hen.' She looked at his face and smiled. 'But thanks for asking.'

He locked the car and they were walking to the stair entry door when it opened and Mia, his next-door neighbour came out with her little dog.

'Hi, Harry. Hey, Alex.' She looked puzzled. 'You look like you've been in the wars.'

'I was in a car accident,' Alex said.

'Oh dear. I'm glad it wasn't too serious. I hope you feel better soon.'

'Thank you.'

'Hopefully your girlfriend will be able to help out.'

Harry and Alex both looked at her. 'Vanessa?'

'Is that her name?'

'The one I described to you earlier.'

'Oh, no, not her. The young blonde one.'

'She was here again?' he said, feeling his heart beat faster.

'Not *was*. Still is. She just opened the door to your flat a minute ago.'

'You wait here,' he said to Alex.

'Like hell I will.'

'I mean it, Alex.' He fished out the car keys and pressed them into her hand. 'Mia, please stay down here for a moment.' He turned back to Alex. 'If you hear a commotion, call treble nine then call Karen Shiels.'

'I can't let you go up there alone.'

'You can and you will.'

'Jesus. I don't like this at all.'

'Please. Just stay here. There's somebody in my flat and she's going to damn well tell me what's going on.' He handed her the fish and chips and went towards the stairs. It was well-lit and he climbed the stone steps as quietly as he could, knowing that the woman could lean out from above and open fire on him, if she was armed.

Why would she be armed? he thought, climbing higher.

He reached the next landing and started making his way up to his own landing on the top floor. Step by step. If the person who was in here was responsible for hurting Alex, she was going to bloody prison.

Staying alert, he reached the landing and approached his front door. He took the key out but then tried the handle. It turned easily and the door opened.

Inside was dark, but he knew the place like the back of his hand, so he didn't need the light.

Where would the woman be waiting?

He walked slowly forward towards the living room door. It was ajar. Could it be a trap?

He suddenly rushed forward, slamming the door open and switching the light on. Then he stopped.

The woman was sitting on his couch.

'Hello, Harry,' she said. 'You look like you've seen a ghost.'

TWENTY-SEVEN

James McCallum sat in front of his large screen TV and played a game on his Xbox.

'Don't you get enough of that?' the female said, putting her hands on his shoulders.

'What? I like playing games.'

'It's too much like work.'

He laughed. 'Can you pour me a drink please?'

'Scotch?'

'What else?'

She squeezed his shoulder before walking over to the drinks cabinet and poured two glasses of single malt. Added ice from the little bucket.

'Oh, would you look at that? I got shot from behind. I hate when that happens.'

'Are you playing with other people online?'

'Yes,' he said. 'My nemesis took me out. I'll have to

have a word with him.' McCallum smiled as he took the glass from her. 'What do you fancy for dinner?'

'I quite fancy that little Italian restaurant in Rose Street. The new place that just opened up. How about it?'

'I better forget about this, then.' He sniffed the whisky and put it on a side table. 'Are they still in the hotel?'

'Yes. I checked.'

'Check again, please.'

She took her phone out and opened the scanner app. 'Max's phone is still saying it's there in the room, even though he's switched it off now.'

McCallum laughed. 'He's such a clown. I wonder what he's going to do when Melissa gets fed up with him?'

'His good looks will see him through.'

'Should I be getting jealous now?' He smiled at her.

'Of course not. Blue talks the talk, but he's as dumb as a log. Yes, he has friends in high places, but only because of his father. Otherwise, nobody would look twice at him.'

'My wife looked twice at him.' His smiled faded and he looked down at the carpet.

'Don't let her get you down. After tomorrow, it will all be over.'

'And yet, tomorrow almost never came. You know, when I started out in this business, I knew there were a lot of people who would want to stand in my way, do whatever it took to destroy me, but I never saw it coming from my wife.'

'As you said, it will all be over tomorrow. They will see for themselves, and then we'll be able to move on.'

'I didn't think she would resort to murder.'

'I have to admit, I was surprised by that as well,' she said. 'And now Dave Pierce is dead too. I'm glad this is going to be over.'

James McCallum stood up from the chair he had been sitting in. He smiled at his companion. 'If Melissa could see me now.'

'How are the knees holding up?'

'Fine. The medical team are keeping quiet with the huge bonuses we're giving them. Just wait 'til we unleash this on the world. You did a marvellous job with the software.'

'The benefits of working from home.'

'You're an absolute genius. And I am so glad that Melissa is only my girlfriend and not my wife on paper. I don't know why she insisted on calling herself my wife.'

'She wanted you all to yourself, James. But I want the real deal. I want it signed on paper.'

He walked over to her on legs that were even more

steady than they had been before he'd had the accident. 'Of course. I want you beside me. We're a team. We're going to take the world by storm.'

'That's good to hear. I have so many more ideas. Now get ready. I'm starved.'

Maggie Carlton walked out of the living room in the big house in the Bush Estate. She loved James more than anything, and nobody, not even Melissa whatever her real last name was, would stand in her way now.

TWENTY-EIGHT

Harry stood looking at the woman. Young, blonde, slim. Just like Mia his neighbour had said.

'Hello, Bea,' he said.

Bea Anderson stood up and smiled. 'Go and tell Alex it's safe to come up. I won't bite. I'm not really dead.'

Harry wasn't sure for a moment, but he took his phone out anyway and sent a text to Alex, his eyes flicking up and down from the screen as his fingers hit the digital keys. He hoped Apple reconfigured what he'd typed, and autocorrected properly.

He surmised that it had as he heard Alex coming up the stairs.

'Jesus,' she said, seeing Bea in the living room.

'I suppose that is an appropriate response, considering I did come back from the dead.'

'You want some chips?' Harry said, nodding to the brown wrapper Alex was holding.

'No, but you two go ahead. I'll put the kettle on though.'

She walked through to the kitchen and Harry raised his eyebrows at Alex; *run now, or get the hammer and stake out?*

'I know it's getting a bit late for coffee, but I think we might need it.' She opened a cupboard and took the mugs out.

'Should I be worried that you know where my mugs are?' Harry said, putting the wrappers on the table and fetching some plates. The little bistro table at the living room window was only designed for two, and Harry was glad of that. It would only take Vanessa to drive by and see *two* women in his flat and she would go home and take some pills.

'We saw you being taken from the mortuary,' Alex said as they were sitting down, eating.

'We thought we'd knocked the cameras out, and for the most part, we did. But there must have been cameras that weren't on the circuit.'

'Correct,' Harry said, tucking into his fish and chips. 'I'm more concerned about who you and your friends are and what's going on.'

Bea had her hands cupped round her coffee. 'I won't tell you my real name, as that will only complicate things. Just keep using my cover name. But we work for British Intelligence. I've been working undercover for a few months now.'

'Who are you investigating?' Alex asked.

'McCallum Technology.'

'The helicopter crash,' Harry said. 'I read the article you left me and I did some research online. A name jumped out at me: Sean Carlton. I guessed he was related to Fiona and Maggie.'

'Their brother.'

Alex looked puzzled.

Harry explained to her. 'Bea left an envelope here, with a newspaper clipping about a helicopter that went down a few months ago. It crashed into the woods, the pilots died and it was blamed on pilot error.'

'Except it wasn't pilot error,' Alex guessed.

'That's what we've been told.'

'By whom?'

'Fiona Carlton,' Bea said. 'She couldn't accept it was pilot error. You see, her brother and the co-pilot didn't work for the MOD, they worked for McCallum Technology. They were test pilots. She just wouldn't let it go, even after the military deemed it to be an accident. But she worked there as a software engineer, and started digging around. Then she found a flaw. Something didn't add up. Something had changed in the schematics. She had worked on the original team, and she knew for a fact that something had been changed. She then contacted us. The MOD are ready to put a lot of money into the new technology. Planes and heli-copters flying with self-charging battery engines with AI doing all the work. It's the future. But if there's a fault we need to know about it.'

Harry washed his fish down with some coffee. 'And that's when you were hired, working undercover.'

'Yes. It was a slow process. I couldn't go trampling in there.'

'How come they didn't find out you were in the government and didn't know the first thing about computers?' Alex asked.

Bea smiled. 'I was chosen because I am a computer expert. I studied software engineering before I joined British Intelligence, that's why I was hand-picked. They couldn't send somebody in blindly.'

'So what next?' Harry asked.

'Fiona made contact with one of the other team members, Dave Pierce. She trusted him. His girlfriend was a friend of Fiona's too. Linda Smith was also a police officer. They got her involved, told her some-thing was going on. Linda had aspirations of being a detective.'

'When we found Fiona, she had Linda's warrant card on her.'

'It was arranged for Linda to park her car in the

Ocean Terminal shopping centre, and Dave put a mask on and broke into the car and stole her uniform. Fiona had ideas about wearing it, since they were about the same size, but then Linda got cold feet. Fiona just used Linda's warrant card after that.'

'Talking of which,' Alex said, 'what about the fake warrant card in my name that was found on you?'

'Sorry. But after you became involved, I had my team make up a copy of yours. It was a real one, just a duplicate of yours.'

Harry pushed his plate away, finished with his dinner. 'McCallum must have been on to you to have somebody try and kill you after killing Fiona.'

Bea put a hand up to her forehead. 'Christ, that hurt. He came in and whacked me. I thought it was one of my team. They were going to meet me at the house. I just thought they were early. I had gone to Maggie Carlton's house to have a look around. Fiona said she had a room full of articles and cuttings. I wanted to see it.'

'Then you were attacked and left for dead,' Alex said.

'Yes. Luckily my team turned up. The house was already on fire but I said to leave me in the house. It would look better if I was dead. One of the team gave me something to render me unconscious and then he turned up after the fire brigade took me out. Then he was right there, before they started doing CPR, and he declared me dead. Then the mortuary van took me away. Scariest thing that's ever happened to me, and then being put in the fridge.'

'That was a brave thing to do.'

Bea shrugged.

'What about the post-mortem you lot did on Fiona?'

'That was my boss's idea. It was a necessity. We had to check to see if she'd swallowed it. It was nasty, but it had to be done.'

'What about those guys breaking into my house?' Alex said.

'I obviously heard you saying you were going to take it so we had to have it. Fiona said she had some of the schematics on there, and the one that had been changed had been put onto a flash drive. He was going to meet her the night she died. To give her the flash drive. He had a room in a hotel. He was paranoid that he would be followed home after the meeting, so he wanted the hotel room to go back to. But he panicked at the handover and ran. Fiona wasn't about to let things go tits up, so she drove after him, and then chased him. He gave it to her in the hotel room. One of my team was there. After we saw Dave running, we got to the hotel, but Fiona had neglected to tell him that we were working with them. It was only after he'd given

Fiona the flash drive did he realise we were on their side. But by then, it was too late.'

'But the bad guys caught her and killed her anyway.' Harry looked at her. 'Then they thought they'd killed you and now they've killed Dave too. Getting rid of the people they thought could bring them down.'

'It looks that way.'

'Did your people inflate my car tyres?' Alex asked.

'No. Why?'

'Because somebody did. And then my car was taken over. Just like Harry's was today when we were at the Bush Estate.'

'I know. I only heard a little while ago. That's why I knew I had to come here. Are you okay?'

'Yes. But I think today in Harry's car was a dry run. Tonight was the real thing. They're trying to kill us. I think we're starting to unravel something that went wrong at McCallum Technology and now they'll do anything, even resort to killing police officers.'

'Have you spoken to Maggie Carlton?' Harry asked.

'No.'

'She moved into the apartment.'

'I know. We wanted to put her into protection, but she wouldn't hear of it. We'll watch her. One of our team will follow her to and from work. We think Max

Blue is involved in this, but he stays on the property at Bush House, and we have every exit covered. The McCallums are still there and so is Blue. If they leave, we'll know about it.'

Harry looked at her then stood up. 'That mark on your head. Can I have a look?'

'Sure. It's where he hit me. God knows what he hit me with but it was enough to knock me out.'

Harry stepped closer and looked at it.

It looked like an eye.

TWENTY-NINE

Alex was stiff and sore when she got up next morning.

'How did you sleep?' Harry asked.

'Like I'd been in a car accident.'

'You should take the rest of the day off. I'm getting the rest of the team to come with me to McCallum Technology. And a whole scrum of uniforms. There's no bastard going to be touching any cars today. I want that arsehole Blue to come to the station for an interview. The PF is drawing up the search warrant right now. I was just on the phone with her.'

'You think I'm going to be in the house watching TV while you're out there having all the fun. I don't think so. I want to look that bastard Blue in the eye and slap the cuffs on him.'

They'd discussed the arrest warrant with Norma Banks, the procurator fiscal, and although they couldn't conclusively point the finger at Max Blue, they had enough to bring him in under suspicion.

'Okay. I made you a coffee. Once you're ready, we can get going.'

'I'll get showered and dressed. I won't be long.'

Half an hour later they were out the door and at the office.

They were all there, including a couple of detective constables from regular CID.

'For those of you who don't know, DS Maxwell's car was hijacked by remote last night. Some of you might have read about cars being taken over and the driver losing all input. This happened last night. We have an idea who is responsible, as it also happened to my car yesterday, while myself and DS Maxwell were leaving the McCallum facility. We think they're playing games, trying to warn us off. And for some reason, they think it's going to work. We're all going to show them today that it isn't. Any questions so far?'

A young female DC put her hand up. 'How do we know for sure this company is behind it?'

'Early this morning, I had a phone call from one of the techs who was looking through my burnt-out car, and they found a little box that had been placed magnetically to the engine bay of my car. Whilst the fire destroyed most of the box, there was a little fragment of motherboard left. With the name McCallum

Technology microscopically engraved near some of the little capacitors. It was a very complex little box, but having that name there means they were involved. So if there's no other questions, let's go get the bastards.'

They were getting into their cars and vans, preparing to go on the drive to the Bush Estate, when Harry got another call. This time it was from one of the forensics team.

'Sir, we found something interesting in the room at Dave Pierce's flat. Where the computer was located.'

Simon Gregg was driving, while in the car behind was Karen Shiels and the new girl Eve Bell.

'What was it?' he asked the man.

'Splinters of wood. Underneath the computer desk, like somebody had broken something wooden over the corner of the desk.'

'Like what?'

'Not sure yet. But on one side of the wood was dark veneer.'

'Thanks for letting me know. Call me again if you narrow it down.'

As they drove up the road in a convoy, something was niggling away inside Harry's brain. Wood. Veneer. What the hell?

THIRTY

'This is it,' Melissa McCallum said to Max Blue. Her name wasn't McCallum but she had called herself that ever since she got entangled with James. Thank God she hadn't legally married him.

'Now that the shares are rock bottom, we can make a killing,' Blue said. 'And then we can move into our own place. I mean, this little house on the property has been fine, but I want to get the hell out of here.'

Melissa smiled. 'Don't worry. It will soon be over.'

'Where's James?'

'He left early this morning. He took a train to London. I knew he had this trip planned, to try and whip up some interest in getting investors of his own, not knowing we were going behind his back.'

'The fool. He doesn't know we're going to pull the rug out from under him.'

198

'Just concentrate on the job at hand, Max. The investors are here.'

'Okay.'

They were in her office in the lab above the underground testing facility. 'Let's go down and meet them.'

Downstairs, the three women and two men were talking to one of the engineers. They turned when Melissa and Max entered.

'Good morning, everybody,' Melissa said. 'I trust you slept well?' She smiled at them. They had better have slept well. The rooms at the Balmoral on Princes Street were costing them a fortune.

'Yes, thank you,' one of the women said. She was very rich, and very powerful. She lived in Washington, DC, close to the Pentagon. 'Can we get on with the demonstration?'

Melissa smiled. 'Of course. My partner, Max, has gone down to the testing facility. He is going to be part of the demonstration, then we can go to the conference room where we can discuss business.'

'I'm looking forward to it.'

Of course you are, Melissa thought. You're going to invest in a company that will be worth billions after this.

They stepped over to the viewing window and Melissa gave the nod to the head engineer, who in turn spoke to his head technician.

'Through there, you will see two adjacent tunnels at each end. We have a train system running in a large loop, something like the New York subway. When the train comes out, you will see our new technology at work. If you look at the screens, you'll see a bird's-eye, 3D view, to give you a clearer picture. But from this viewing window, we can see directly across the level crossing.

The saw Max Blue walk over to a small car. He turned around, smiled and waved at them.

Then he got in the car.

'Max is a genius,' she said, smiling. 'He has brought so much to the technology in this company.'

'I just hope he knows what he's doing,' the woman replied.

Max started the car and drove it up onto the railway track.

'Those tracks are almost identical to the steel ones of old, but they are made of stronger material and filled with sensors. If a car is fitted with one of our retro-fit sensors, it will talk to the train. If it's an old car, then the train will be talking to the rails, and the rails will know if a car has passed over one set but not the other. Then all sorts of cameras come into play, but even if the train is working autonomously, it will know to stop. And here's our demonstration today, which we can watch, and then we can go and show you footage of some other applications of the AI we designed.'

'Does that car have the AI in it?' the woman asked.

'Yes, it does. This is the brand new autonomous vehicle that we hope to have running on the roads within the next two years. Way ahead of the competition.'

They all stood and watched the huge arena below.

———

Max Blue drove the car onto the tracks. The software had been calibrated to perfection, he had seen to it himself, and what better way to demonstrate his confidence in the technology than to be a part of the demonstration himself.

Then his phone rang. Who the hell was this?

'This is a bad time,' he said to the as-yet unknown caller.

'Max! James here! How are you enjoying your little stunt?'

'James? What's going on?'

McCallum laughed. 'Why don't you tell them, old friend? No, wait, do let me tell you; the train that is going through the loop right now is gathering speed, and I have had its brain switched off.'

'What are you talking about?'

'Let me explain. I know what you did to the engine system on that helicopter. You killed those pilots. You had the investors running to the hills, didn't you Max? You and my girlfriend. You know the one, she calls herself Melissa McCallum although we were never married. You don't think she wants you, Max, do you?'

'You're delusional, James.'

'Am I? I don't think so. You see, I found out about your investors. Once my stock had tanked, which it did, then your investors would jump in, buy up my company, then when the military contracts came back, the share prices would go through the roof. Especially after you announce the self-driving cars are ready to go.'

'I'm not going to listen to this, James. You're finished. This is going to be our company by the day's end.'

'I want you to admit you tampered with the software on that helicopter, killing those people.'

'Or what?'

'The train has just entered the part of the loop where it's turned and is now facing you. In three minutes, the train will enter the tunnel and accelerate towards you. I have had my best engineer remotely take over the project. Nothing you can do at Bush will be able to stop it. The car has also been remotely taken over. You can't drive it or unlock it, and thanks to our anti-theft measures, you can't smash your way out of it. You have around four minutes to live, Max. The train will be doing over a hundred when it hits you. This is your choice. Detective Chief Inspector Harry McNeil is up in the viewing area waiting. If you tell him, then the train will stop.'

'You asshole. My lawyer will get me off. I'm confessing under duress.'

'Wrong again. Your digital footprints are all over that helicopter crash. Hard to find, unless you know what to look for, but luckily for me, I have somebody on my team who does.'

'You're bluffing.'

'Am I? Well, we'll let Chief Inspector McNeil sort that out, will we? After the train hits the car.'

'He'll know this is murder.'

'He can't hear anything right now. But I'm about to switch the screen on. Oh, and when they look, they'll see you were the last one to calibrate the software. My engineer will cover her own tracks, by replicating your digital imprint. Just like you did to bring the helicopter down. Five seconds, then McNeil will see you. And so will I. Your choice, Max.'

He pulled and pulled at the car's door handle but it wouldn't budge.

He shook his head. 'Go to hell. McCallum.'

Five seconds later, the little screen in the car

showed him the view the others were getting up in the control room.

He opened a laptop and plugged it in to a USB in the car. He started typing furiously.

And in that second, Melissa could see her whole future going up in smoke.

Harry McNeil and the other officers were watching Max Blue hacking away at the keyboard on the laptop.

'What's he doing?' Harry asked.

Melissa turned to him. 'There's only one reason he'd be battering away at that laptop; he's trying to stop the train. Something's gone wrong.'

There was a kill switch in front of her, a big, red button that she could smack her hand down onto, but she knew if she did that, then the whole thing was over.

But she knew it was all over anyway.

The lights from the train were visible as it started its countdown towards the level crossing where Max Blue sat.

Melissa slammed her hand down on the big, red button.

And nothing happened.

The lights kept coming. She turned to the chief engineer sitting at a desk a few feet away.

'Stop that train!'

'I can't!' he shouted back at her. 'Blue's just overridden the emergency software. Jesus.'

'Well, you override that!'

'I can't. I've been locked out.'

'Oh my God,' Alex said in a low voice as they got a view from inside the train cab. It was turning at the end of the loop before making its journey down to the level crossing.

'How long before that train hits?' Harry asked.

'What?' Melissa said.

'How long before the bloody train hits the car?' he shouted at her.

'Three minutes, maybe less if he ramps up the speed. Two minutes maybe. Why?'

Harry ran to the door that said *Authorised Personnel Only* and opened it, feeling the change in the air. It was colder here. He turned around, looking for what he'd seen through the window.

Alex was right on his heels. 'Harry, what are you doing?' she screamed at him.

'Get back in there!' He ran to a door marked *Maintenance*. A man was sitting inside.

'Your van keys! Where are they?'

The man was flabbergasted for a second. 'In the ignition,' he said.

The Transit sat back away from the track, a white vehicle with red and yellow chevrons painted on it. He jumped in behind the wheel and started it up. He could see the lights from the train.

He floored the van, going over the first crossing. The barriers were down on the second one but he drove through them and hit the back of the car full tilt, smashing it off the track. The van stalled after the airbags deployed. Harry looked and saw the train bearing down on him.

The van wouldn't start.

THIRTY-ONE

For Alex, everything went into slow motion. She ran after Harry as he went into the small office. Then he came back out again, shouting at her but she couldn't hear what he said. Then she saw him jump into the van and start it up. What the hell was he doing?

Then she realised what he was doing, but she couldn't quite grasp why.

The van was moving towards the train tracks. It crossed the first level crossing, then smashed through the barriers of the second and crashed into the back of the car, pushing it off the tracks.

Then she saw the lights of the train as it was coming out of the tunnel.

The van stayed on the tracks. It was almost sideways to her and she thought at first that the momentum had carried it off the tracks, but then she saw it was still on.

Alex was shouting and screaming, unaware of the faces that were watching through the viewing window.

The train was approaching fast and still Harry wasn't opening the driver's door. She started running towards the van, over the first level crossing, so focused on the driver's door that she wasn't even aware of the train now.

She started saying Harry's name over and over, her eyes locked onto the driver's door. It wasn't opening. Something must have happened.

Then she saw the figure coming from around the back of the van, running at her. She couldn't see who it was for the tears in her eyes but then the figure was lunging at her.

Was it Max Blue? Jesus, he was coming to kill her and Harry was in the van and the trains was about to kill them all.

THIRTY-TWO

Harry cursed himself. He had knocked the car off the tracks but now he was stuck. The damn seatbelt wouldn't unlock. He yanked at it, pulled and tugged but nothing.

The train was coming. He saw the lights in the tunnel and knew it was bearing down on him.

He took a deep breath and let it out slowly. *Keep calm or else you'll die.* His eyes locked onto the train lights.

He slowly pulled the seatbelt from the shoulder point, easing it through the clip until it was loose on his stomach. With his other hand, he lifted it up higher off his lap and started to pull his legs up. Feeding more belt through the clip, it came a bit higher, then stopped. It had locked in place. He eased it up more, now not even wanting to see the train. If he looked, he'd panic and then it would be over.

He fed a little bit more through, then he was pushing with one hand and he got his legs up and they were out past the lap portion of the seatbelt, and he was suddenly lying halfway onto the passenger seat.

He pushed and kicked and broke free of the seatbelt and his hand was reaching for the door handle, He pushed himself at the same time, his body shoving against the door and then he was falling out.

That's when he saw Alex shouting and screaming. Other people running through the doorway. The new girl, Eve, in front, Karen behind and the big lumbering giant that was Simon Gregg, followed by uniforms.

Alex was approaching the track. She couldn't see him. He ran then, ran faster than he had in a long time and threw himself at Alex as the train's lights came bearing down on them.

THIRTY-THREE

No more than five feet, Harry thought as he sat up. The train had stopped no more than five feet from the van.

'Jesus,' he said, his body aching. Then he looked at Alex sprawled beside him, the other team members running up to them. 'You okay?' he said to Alex.

'I'm fine. Sore, but fine.' She sat up and was helped to her feet by Gregg.

'Lying down on the job? You'll get written up for that,' he said, grinning.

'Shut up,' she said.

Then they watched as Eve Bell came across with Max Blue, shaken but not badly hurt.

'How did that train not smash into the van?' he said.

'Get him out of here,' Harry said as he stood up.

Inside, James McCallum was standing up out of his wheelchair, his face beaming. He turned to the other people who were rooted to the spot. 'And ladies and gentlemen, that concludes the physical part of the test.'

'What just happened, McCallum?' Harry said.

'You mean, me being able to walk, or...'

'The train. Explain what just happened.'

'As you can see, the train stopped. My engineers lied for Melissa's benefit. We had everything under control. Melissa had these good people invited here, thinking they were the investors, or at least people representing the investors. But they're not. They're from the MOD, working undercover. They went through everything yesterday, and found what Max Blue did to the system on board the helicopter to bring it down.

'Melissa and Max had sabotaged the helicopter by replacing one of the parts, which Max then manipulated, causing the 'copter to crash. As a result, my shares went through the basement. He and Melissa wanted to get their own investors to snap up the stock at rock bottom prices. And it almost worked. Until we had our own meeting.

'I told them that they would be working with a couple of murderers. I assured them I had fixed everything and the train would run perfectly. That's why when I cornered Max and tried to get him to confess, he thought he could go ahead and manipulate the system. As you can see, my top engineer and I had already put the new system in place. I just wanted to give the MOD a true demonstration. It was all a bluff. The train was going to stop. And you know Max will try and pin all of this on you, Melissa.'

'That will be right. I'll tell McNeil there anything he wants to know,' she said before being led out.

McCallum turned to the MOD people. 'So, you saw for yourself, even with somebody like Max Blue's knowledge, the system couldn't be overridden. That train wasn't going to hit his car.'

Harry looked at Alex. 'Thanks for trying to help me anyway.'

'Right back at you. You thought the train was going to hit the van.'

The lead female investigator walked up to McCallum. 'We had reservations about Melissa. We put Bea Anderson in place after Fiona contacted us, and Bea confirmed what we suspected; that Max Blue was a master manipulator. Thank you for showing us you've got things under control. I think I speak for all of us when I say we will be using you, Mr McCallum.'

'Thank you.'

'What about the legs?' Harry said to McCallum.

The man smiled. 'That's another thing we have to

discuss. Not only the automotive world, but the medical world too.'

Harry nodded. 'Who's the engineer you were talking about? I thought Fiona Carlton was your best engineer?'

'She was. But she had an equal. Her sister, Maggie. She's helped me through all of this. She and her sister were both friends with Dave Pierce's girlfriend. God rest his soul.'

'And Melissa had them murdered.'

Melissa turned to him. 'I know those pilots died because of us, but I'm not taking the blame for those murders. Fiona Carlton and Dave Pierce being murdered wasn't anything to do with us. We never touched them.'

Harry watched her back as they were led away.

'Do you believe her?' Alex said.

'I think I do.' Splinters. Veneer. 'Christ.'

'What is it?'

'I need to call Bea Anderson.'

THIRTY-FOUR

He walked along the side of the canal, just another punter out for a walk. Brisk, autumn day. Nothing out of the ordinary. People passed him by but didn't give him another look.

He walked along to the gardens that were in front of the entrances that overlooked the canal basin. He took out the keys he'd acquired and opened the front door. Inside, he approached the front door of the apartment with confidence. This was the last one.

The front door opened quietly. The apartment itself was deadly quiet. He closed the front door and walked quietly up to the living room. He didn't know if she would be in here or not, but considering what time of day it was, there was a good chance.

And he was right.

'Hello, Maggie,' he said to the young blonde woman.

She turned around. 'Hello. But my name's not Maggie.'

'Oh, I'm sorry,' he said, about to turn and leave. 'I was to meet her here. I got a call saying she knew who killed my daughter.'

'I know.' Bea Anderson smiled. 'That was me.'

'What's going on?'

'I think you know what's going on, Mr Smith,' Harry said from behind.

'I don't understand,' Brian Smith said, leaning heavily on his medical walking stick.

'I think you understand perfectly well. Are you really disabled?'

'You're about to find out.'

Harry thought Smith was going to attack him with the stick but he turned his attention to Bea instead. He brought the stick up and was about to bring it down but Bea was prepared this time and stepped in to meet the stick and she pulled Smith over and twisted his arm back.

The big, bald man she worked with ran into the room and roughly manhandled Smith into a chair, taking his walking stick away from him.

'Move, and I'll bend this over your head. You hear?' he said to Smith.

Smith said nothing as the big man stepped to one side.

'Why?' Harry said, grateful the big man had stepped in. He was aching in joints he hadn't realised he had.

'They deserved it. Getting my Linda involved in that caper. They caused her death! If it wasn't for them, she wouldn't be dead! So, yes, I killed that stupid bitch Fiona Carlton, and Dave Pierce.'

'And you thought you'd killed Bea here.'

'Whoever the hell she is. Yes, I thought I'd killed Maggie Carlton. I couldn't let the three of them get away with killing my daughter.'

Maggie Carlton walked into the room. 'I am so sorry about Linda, but you didn't bring her back by killing my sister, or Linda's boyfriend.'

'Is that where you got the key for this place?' Harry asked.

He nodded. 'It was Fiona's. I took the keys from her the night I murdered her. But you lot deserved it. You might not have been driving the van, but you had her working in her spare time. Working on this stupid conspiracy theory you had going.'

Harry stood next to Maggie. 'Why don't you tell them the truth, Brian?'

'What do you mean?' He looked at Harry with undisguised contempt.

'Tell them you were the one driving the taxi that night.'

Maggie looked puzzled. 'What are you talking about?'

Smith looked at her before answering. 'I don't know what's he's talking about.'

'Because of her injuries, where she was struck on her hip, they thought that she had been hit by a van,' Harry said. 'Dave Pierce got it wrong that night. He said he saw a van driving away. He hadn't seen the accident happen, but when he got into the street, he saw a van driving far away up the road with no lights on. This is what he reported,' Harry said.

'Is this true?' Maggie asked.

'Are you going to listen to him? The police couldn't catch her killer, so he's trying to come up with some cockamamie story about it being me.'

Harry continued. 'When we were in your house the other day, I saw a little leather pouch with a drawstring. I thought it was some kind of cosh at first, but then I remembered a friend of mine years ago had one. It's a little bag that a taxi driver carries his change in. It opens quickly and spreads out. Then you pull the drawstring. But you're disabled, Mr Smith. You couldn't be driving a taxi surely? But I had one of my detectives contact cab companies, and we narrowed it down to one company in particular where an owner had his taxi off the road a few months ago, because his driver said a van had backed into it, smashing the front wing. But it wasn't a van, was it Mr Smith? It was your daughter striking the front of your taxi that caused the damage. The owner confirmed that you rent a cab from him. Working on the side whilst claiming benefits.'

His head slumped for a second, before it came shooting back up. 'If you people hadn't got her involved, she would still be alive.'

'If you weren't a benefits cheat, she would still be alive,' Harry countered.

'How did you know he was going to come for me?' Maggie asked.

'He knew he hadn't killed you in your house. He set fire to it anyway, thinking whoever he had hit was dead. But it was the mark on Bea's head. Fiona had the same one. It's in the shape of an eye. I thought it was very strange, and I was puzzled as to what would make such a mark. Then I remembered Smith there had a fancy walking stick when I first met him. One with a duck's head. He used it to hit your sister with, to stun her before stabbing her. Same with Bea, but I think he didn't want to use the same MO. Just hit her and then let the fire take care of the rest. Then I assume you were told by Pierce that Maggie was still alive?'

Smith nodded.

'What about Dave?' Maggie said.

'He would have had the same mark probably, but I think the sharp duck's beak caught him, rather than the duck's face. And then something happened, and the walking stick broke on Dave's desk. Forensics found some splinters with veneer on them. It was from the walking stick, wasn't it, Mr Smith?'

'Yes.' Smith answered.

'That's when I saw him with the medical walking stick. I couldn't be sure, mind, but I had a good idea.'

Maggie shook her head. 'He killed his own daughter in an accident, then he blames us for it.'

'He tried to convince himself that he wasn't to blame. But this is all on you, Mr Smith.' Harry walked over to him.

'You're under arrest. Stand up.'

THIRTY-FIVE

'What's this?' Alex said, putting two plates down on the little table in the living room. 'More car brochures?'

'I'm still window shopping.' He looked up at her. 'What about you? Another Beemer?'

She sat down opposite him. They were waiting for the Chinese to be delivered.

'I'm not sure. I'm thinking of something different now. Don't laugh, but I'm thinking of getting one of the new Honda CR-Vs.'

'Now you're just having me on.'

She laughed. 'I'm not. They're great wee cars.'

'I know. I mean, so I heard. But we can't have the same car.'

'What about your classic?'

'The parts should be in soon, but it's not a car I'd

like to go out driving in the winter. I might just stick with the ratty old pool car for now.'

'What? Away with yourself.'

'There's no rush. Maybe I'll get a Mercedes.'

'That's too posh.'

'One of those big, four by four things.'

'You know nothing about cars, do you?'

'I'm learning.'

'I'll take you car shopping. Just so you won't embarrass yourself by buying a hairdresser's car.'

He smiled at her as they looked out the window, waiting for the delivery driver to call them to say he couldn't find the address.

'I can get my stuff together and move back along the road,' she said. 'Now that this case is over.'

'Whenever. No rush. I mean, I don't want you to think I'm kicking you out.'

'I know. Maybe at the weekend? I know you hurt yourself this morning throwing yourself at me, and I know it's been a long time since a man threw himself at me...'

'Here's the Chinese,' he replied. 'Throwing myself at you. If you'd bloody well done as I told you and stayed where you were...'

AFTERWORD

A few things got the ball rolling for this book. I'm a car guy, and I find it fascinating that one day – maybe not in my time – cars will be driving themselves, with very little input from humans while the car is driving. I read articles about the test cars being hit by cars being driven by humans, because we basically don't obey the law and stop at stop signs and the like.

I've watched videos on YouTube about inventors who built engines that don't need petrol (gas) to run on, and I firmly believe that an alternative engine exists, but the big oil companies won't reveal them, but the patents are snapped up and made to disappear.

I was reading about helicopter crashes one day, and started thinking about why nobody talks about electric engines in aircraft, so I included that aspect in the book. The mention of a helicopter crash wasn't based on any one incident.

Now I'd like to thank my advance readers for their support. You are all wonderful. A special thanks to Eve. And a very big thank you to my editor, Melanie Underwood, who once again stepped up and knocked it out the park.

And thanks to you, the reader, for coming along on this journey. If I could ask you for a big favour – if you could leave a review for this book and any other of mine, that would be terrific. I appreciate each and ever one.

John Carson
New York
October 2019

ABOUT THE AUTHOR

John Carson is originally from Edinburgh but now lives with his wife and family in New York State.

website - johncarsonauthor.com
    Facebook - JohnCarsonAuthor
    Twitter - JohnCarsonBooks
    Instagram - JohnCarsonAuthor